A TAIL OF WOE

A WHISKERS AND WORDS MYSTERY
BOOK FIVE

ERYN SCOTT

KRISTOPHERSON
PRESS
Publishing

In this Christmas story, there is no happy ending for Scrooge.

Louisa Henry has read the Dickens classic enough times to spot a Scrooge when she sees one. Arthur Crawford is as sour as they come. Even worse? There's no chance for his redemption because during the town's Christmas tree lighting, his body is found suspended in the lights of the largest pine.

No one is surprised that Arthur's selfish ways finally caught up with him. But when it becomes apparent that the killer won't stop, Lou must delve deep into Arthur's Christmases past to find out who took away his Christmas future.

Welcome to Button
BOBBIN RD.
PATTERN DR.
BIAS RD.
Jr. High
YARD RD.
Elem.
11
NEEDLE ST.
RIBBON RD.
High School
STITCH ST.
SPOOL AVE.
SPOOL AVE.
3
8
Antiques
7
6
BBQ
1
2
THIMBLE DR.
THREAD LN.
THREAD LN.
10
PIN ST.
PATTERN DR.
BINDING ST.
Police
Pizza
5
Vet Clinic
9
Outdoor Eq.
4
LINEN DR.
Theater
Hospital
Grocery Store
NEEDLE ST.
TEXTILE RD.
HEM AVE.
Button Lake
Auto Repair
Hardware
Lumber
Storage
NEEDLE ST.

1 - Whiskers and Words   4 - George's Technology Emporium   7 - Button Bistro
2 - Material Girls   5 - Bean and Button Coffehouse   8 - Pet Store   9 - Bakery
3 - Willow and Easton's houses   6 - The Upholstered Button   10- Old Mansion
11- Willow's Nursery

CHAPTER 1

Louisa Henry peered out the front window of her bookshop, Whiskers and Words. Her breath fogged the pane of cold glass, obstructing her view. She frowned and used the sleeve of her sweater to buff away the steam before stepping back to pace around the shop.

A sweet meow caught her attention, and she stopped by a table where a white cat woke from his morning nap. Sapphire, named for the bright blue color of his jewel tone eyes, stretched and blinked up at his owner. Lou kissed the cat's head, scrunching her fingers into the soft fur by his collar that read Not for Adoption. While Sapphy wasn't the only cat who called Whiskers and Words home, he was its only permanent resident. The other cats that lounged around the bookshop were up for adoption, on the lookout for their forever homes.

A knock at the shop door behind Lou made her jump in surprise. She deflated when she saw it was her best friend, Willow.

It wasn't as if Lou was unhappy to see her friend—the two of them had been inseparable since they met in second grade—

but she saw Willow practically every day now that they lived in the same small town, and Willow wasn't who Lou was eager to see.

"No sightings yet?" Willow asked when Lou let her inside.

Lou shook her head. Her parents were set to arrive that morning. They would stay for the entire month of December, and Lou couldn't be more excited.

Willow pulled off her wool gloves and cupped her hands over her mouth to warm them. It hadn't snowed yet that winter, but from the chilly temperature and billowing clouds covering the gray sky, Lou wondered whether they might get their first dusting that day.

She was torn between being excited for it to snow and wanting the roads to be safe for her parents' arrival. They were driving a large RV, but they were coming from Montana, so she knew they'd encountered snow before and were well equipped. Caroline and Bruce Welsh had retired about a year and a half ago. After selling their home and buying the RV of their dreams, they'd started checking locations off of their travel wish list.

"Dad texted, saying they were driving through Brine," Lou told Willow as she continued her nervous pacing. "They should be here any minute."

"I haven't had a Bruce and Care Bear Christmas in ... years." Willow wiggled her fingers in excitement.

While Caroline's work friends often shortened her name to Caro, Willow was the only person who'd ever been able to get away with referring to Caroline by the nickname Care Bear. It had started when Willow was seven and was obsessed with the colorful cartoon bears, so Caroline had let it slide.

Lou blinked. "That's right. I keep forgetting you haven't seen them in a while since they came to New York last year to help me pack."

Louisa's husband, Ben, had passed away two summers ago, right at the beginning of her parents' retirement. They'd flown to New York to be with Lou, helping her with the funeral, getting Ben's affairs in order, and lending general emotional support. They couldn't stay forever, though, and had eventually gone back to Washington to sell their house and start their life of full-time travel, only returning the week of Christmas when Lou had been packing up her condo to move.

Time had gone by so quickly, Lou realized. She was coming up on her first anniversary of living in Button after moving her whole life across the country.

"It's just too bad *your* parents are going to be gone," Lou mused.

Willow's parents lived an hour south of Button, where Willow and Lou had grown up, and were good friends with Caroline and Bruce. But they were taking a vacation to the sunny shores of Hawaii for the first time in a decade, and Willow was happy they would have time to relax while escaping some of the winter weather.

"I know. I like the sign, by the way." Willow jabbed her thumb over her shoulder, toward the bookshop door.

Lou had taped a sign in the window that said, *Closed for family visit. Thank you for understanding!* She rarely closed on Thursdays but wanted to give her parents her full attention.

The wheeze of an air brake broke through the midmorning quiet. Willow and Lou froze for a moment before rushing to the back door of the bookshop, which let out into the alley. When they opened the door, they saw a large RV taking up the space in between Lou's building and the boutique behind her.

Bruce Welsh came around the large vehicle first. Lou's father was of an average height, with a slight potbelly and a full head of gray hair, punctuated by an equally full mustache. He had a penchant for colorful sweater vests and fancy socks. It was no wonder he loved to dress so brightly—the man had spent most of his career teaching kindergarten, after all.

"Aren't you a sight for sore eyes?" Bruce opened his arms wide and pulled his daughter into one of his signature tight hugs.

Lou wheezed happily as he crushed the air out of her lungs. "Hi, Dad. I think your hugs are tighter than even Willow's," she observed, shooting a grin at her best friend, who was known for her intense way of embracing people.

Bruce let out a deep laugh, pulling back as he held on to Lou's forearms so he could get a better look at her. "It's so good to see you."

"And to be done with driving for a few weeks," Caroline Welsh exited the RV next, pulling Lou into a soft hug as Bruce moved on to greet Willow.

Caroline was a petite woman who—between her khaki hiking pants, eggplant colored long-sleeved shirt, and fleece vest—was dressed like she'd stepped off the pages of an outdoor living magazine. Finishing out her career as a construction supervisor meant that her wardrobe needs were more about durability and comfort rather than fashion but Lou thought her mom always looked lovely. Her graying brown hair was cut into an impeccable bob, matching her playful yet tidy personality.

Lou kissed her mom on the cheek. "If you're sick of driving, I think you might have made a huge mistake by selling your house for an RV," Lou joked.

Caroline shot her daughter an amused smile. "You know what I mean. I love it, but it was a long stretch from Montana."

"I know." Lou let go of her mom so she and Willow could hug.

"Button is adorable, girls." Caroline peeked down to the end of the alleyway they stood in. "I think I got a toothache just driving through downtown."

The town of Button, Washington, was cute on a normal day. Between the quaint businesses, each with colorful window frames, and the sewing-themed streets, it was as *cute as a button*. Being the first day of December, however, the town had strung white Christmas lights along the major thoroughfares, and big red bows adorned the base of each streetlight, making the town look like a wrapped gift.

"Wait until you see the rest of it," Willow said, helping Lou's parents bring their bags inside.

Even though her parents could technically sleep in the RV, Lou had a guest room for them to use. With the cold temperatures approaching, it made sense for them to stay inside. The group of four bustled into the bookshop, leaving the bags by the staircase while Lou gave a tour. She was incredibly proud of her shop, with its cozy feel, comforting scents, and cute winter-themed book displays.

As they walked through, four felines became visible in the space. Caroline and Bruce already knew the deaf white cat sleeping on the table near the front window. Sapphire had lived with Lou back in New York City during her previous life as an editor for a major publishing house. Three cats were new to them, however. Anne Mice was a gray tabby who was as beautiful as she was friendly. Catnip Everdeen was a skittish orange-and-white cat who had a soft spot for one of Lou's regulars, an old man named Silas. Lou's newest arrival, Charles Lickens, was a gorgeous British Blue who'd come to her last week when his owner found out she had to move, and her new apartment wouldn't allow cats.

Lou was more than happy to take in a new resident. That

was what she did. Whiskers and Words wasn't just a bookshop —it doubled as a rescue-cat sanctuary. Not only did Lou give rescue cats a cozy place to stay while they waited for their forever home, but the constant flux of customers in the bookshop gave people plenty of interaction with the cats, often creating a bond that led to an adoption. Their literary names and pleasant personalities didn't hurt the endeavor.

"Oh, honey, it's wonderful. Just like you and Ben always talked about." Caroline wrapped an arm around Lou's shoulders and pulled her tight.

Lou blinked back the tears that pricked at her eyes. It had been their dream to own a bookstore together. In Ben's absence, Lou had made it a reality.

"Can we see upstairs?" Bruce asked.

Together, they clomped up the back staircase to the cozy two-bedroom apartment where Lou lived above the shop. After touring the home—with cats as tour guides, of course—they settled around the dining room table and chatted about their plans.

"First order of business is a trip around town," Willow said, matter-of-factly, a statement with which everyone agreed.

"Then lunch. I'm already hungry." Caroline patted her stomach. "We were on the road before the sun was up today."

"We can definitely take care of that," Lou said. "And we have the town's Christmas tree lighting tonight to kick off the month of December. I know you said you were interested in going to some local holiday events, Mom."

Caroline's eyes went wide. "Yes, I want to hit them all. A Christmas tree lighting sounds like the perfect way to end our first day in town."

Bruce cleared his throat. The three women looked over at him.

"That all sounds great. But we can't possibly forget..." He circled his hands in the air, waiting for one of them to supply the end to his hanging sentence.

"Our ritual watching of *The Princess Bride*," Lou said, a lightness radiating through her chest.

The Princess Bride was Bruce's favorite movie. He and Lou used to watch it every year when she was growing up. Ever since she'd moved to New York City to go to college, they'd made a pact that one of the first things they would do when they saw each other was watch the movie together.

"Don't worry, Dad," Lou added. "We can fit that in between lunch and the Christmas tree lighting. They won't start the lighting until seven."

Caroline and Willow nodded along with the plans. No one was as intense about the movie as Lou and Bruce were, but they appreciated the tradition.

Willow stood. "Well, let's get that tour of downtown started, then."

"Yes," Lou said, following suit. "And we should start the tour with the property for Willow's new nursery."

Caroline's hands flew to her mouth. "I can't wait."

Lou's parents had heard all about Willow leaving her teaching career to open a nursery of her own. Excited, the four of them bustled out the door, bundled up in thick winter jackets, scarves, and gloves.

"As you wish," they all said together as the last line of the movie played later that day.

Bruce stretched, scaring Catnip Everdeen, who'd curled up

in his lap around the halfway mark of the movie. "Sorry, Catnip," he said with a wince.

Lou waved away his worries. The fact that Catnip had sat on him at all meant he was one of the few *chosen ones*, and Lou had a lot of anecdotal proof, mostly surrounding Silas, that once Catnip found someone she loved, nothing could sway her affection. Speaking of affection ... a white paw rested on Lou's shoulder, reminding her that Sapphire was curled up on the back of the couch behind her.

Caroline stood, folding the throw blanket she'd been snuggled up underneath during the movie. Willow yawned, scooting both Anne Mice and Charles Lickens off her lap. Lou glanced out the window. Darkness had fallen over the town of Button, but there was still not a snowflake to be seen. A fire glowed orange behind the glass of Lou's fireplace, keeping them warm, and making Lou wish they could stay inside where it was toasty.

But the promise of her first Christmas season in Button gave her the energy to stand, and she turned off the fireplace. "We should head to the lighting," Lou said, checking the clock.

Her parents mumbled and grabbed their winter jackets while Willow texted someone on her phone. Lou smiled, sure her friend was letting Easton know they were on their way. Willow and Easton, a local detective for the Button Police Department, had been seeing each other for the past few months, and he was going to meet them there.

Well, if the stories Lou had heard about the grand lighting ceremony were to be believed, the whole town would be there. Having moved in during January, Lou had just missed out on the Christmas festivities the previous year. The reminder that parking might be scarce made Lou hurry everyone along. "We want to get a good spot."

They piled into Willow's car and drove the couple of miles down Linen Drive until they reached Button Memorial Park. Not only did the park hold multiple fields for recreational soccer, football, and lacrosse leagues, but it had a castle-themed play structure for the kids, and was flanked by a line of evergreens.

Willow directed them toward the fence along one field. "That's where we'll stand to watch."

Someone had strung Christmas lights along the top of a chain-link fence. The strands emitted a warm glow, and there was already a collection of locals gathered next to the lighted section of fencing, like the people of Button were moths, crowding around a lamp or flame.

"The decorations will be across the field on that grouping of trees there," Willow said, gesturing to looming, tree-shaped shadows across the largest field as she led them over to the viewing area.

As they approached the group of people, Lou recognized the local veterinarian, Noah Romero. He stood next to the tall figure of Easton West. And while Easton pulled Willow into a tight hug, Lou sidled up next to Noah, giving him a wave.

"Hey," he said, his signature dimples just visible in the soft glow of the Christmas lights along the fence. A puff of warm breath accompanied the single word, visible in the frosty night, which made him laugh, causing the billowing cloud to grow larger.

"Noah and Easton, these are my parents, Bruce and Caroline." Lou pivoted and gestured to her parents, standing just behind her. They shook gloved hands and said their hellos before Lou noticed someone was missing. Noah's daughter wasn't standing next to him. "No Marigold?"

Noah shook his head. "She's with Cassidy tonight," he said,

mentioning his ex-wife. "Her parents live in Brine, and they do a pickle lighting, or something quirky like that. Marigold loves those things."

Willow rolled her eyes and explained about the quirky neighboring town to Caroline and Bruce. In that time, more townspeople arrived, filling in the empty spaces along the fence.

All conversations came to a halt as the mayor of Button, Teller Edwards, came around to the other side of the fence, so he was facing the townspeople, his back to the line of trees that was about to be illuminated.

"People of Button, I can't believe we're already almost through another year," the mayor said into a loudspeaker.

Even though it wasn't *that* large of a crowd, and he was standing only ten feet away, he needed the boost in volume. Mayor Edwards reminded Lou of a mouse, with his small stature and quiet voice. Lou had gotten used to New York City mayors, who tended to be loud with larger-than-life personalities; they had to be if they wanted to command the respect of the residents of the Big Apple. But it was just like Button to elect a figurehead who was as unassuming as their small town.

Mayor Edwards continued. "Our own A-Plus Electric donated this year's display. Let's give a round of applause to Arthur Crawford and the electricians at A-Plus."

He paused as the crowd clapped. But instead of being enthusiastic, the applause was hesitant and mixed with confused whispers.

"Did he just say Arthur Crawford did the display this year?" someone behind Lou asked in the pitch black.

Another person answered, saying, "That doesn't sound right. Arthur doesn't do anything for free. Plus, he hates Christmas."

Mayor Edwards's cheeks turned even redder as his eyes flicked nervously over the crowd. Lou wasn't sure if the mayor could clearly hear what the people were saying, but he wouldn't need to in order to sense the disbelief radiating from the people.

He clapped his hands together. "Without further ado, here's your Christmas display. Let's give 'em a countdown from five." The mayor turned, opening his arms toward the trees.

The crowd counted down, "Five! Four! Three! Two! One!"

A transformer buzzed to life somewhere to the left of where the crowd gathered. Electricity hummed through the wires, illuminating an elaborate display. The crowd gasped. Besides the lights draped along the boughs, large snowflakes had been created from blue lights at the base of each tree. White and red lights had been fashioned into candy canes in between.

But it was the display on the tallest of the three trees that was difficult to discern. Was it supposed to be a present?

A scream tore through the frosty night.

A woman to Lou's left pointed and said, "Is someone hanging in the lights?" Her voice shook with terror.

Everyone squinted as they tried to get a closer look at where she pointed.

Sure enough, in the middle tree, the strands of lights toward the bottom had become tangled. They were wrapped around a person. A person who wasn't moving.

The lights cut out as someone turned off the power. The faint glow from the strands of Christmas lights along the fence next to the viewing area became the only reprieve from the darkness once more.

Noah, Easton, and a few other men hopped the fence, racing forward to help. Beams of light illuminated the dark trees as Easton and the others pulled out flashlights to get a better look at the scene. People with young children moved them away or averted their eyes. Lou was suddenly thankful that Marigold hadn't been in attendance.

What remained of the crowd stood there, shivering and waiting as Easton investigated.

"I think he was dead," someone in the crowd whispered.

Bruce leaned closer to Lou and said, "Any chance he was only *mostly* dead?" The hopeful glance her dad gave her after quoting the line from his favorite movie made Lou's heart break.

"Sorry, Dad. I don't think so." Lou curled her lip. "I'm afraid your first day in Button has been marred by a man's death."

CHAPTER 2

The low, worried hum of whispers buzzed through the waiting crowd. The stamping of feet and blowing on icy fingers came to a stop as Easton used his flashlight to inspect the body. The people of Button seemed to hold their breath all at once.

The flashlight beam landed on a man's face as Easton and Noah turned the body around.

"That's Arthur Crawford," a woman with a long purple scarf said.

Gasps arose from the crowd.

"It can't be." A man, who was wearing a Santa hat, let out a derisive snort. Lou had seen him around town but didn't know his name. "Are you joking? Arthur Crawford up in a tree? That guy wouldn't be caught dead doing any manual labor."

"Or paying his workers a fair salary, if he can help it," a man wearing a wool hat with earflaps, named Hayden, chimed in.

Lou, Willow, Caroline, and Bruce huddled closer to the group as they listened.

"No, it really is Arthur." A young man stepped forward. He

wore a bright orange sweatshirt like the guys on Caroline's construction crews used to wear, making him easy to see in the relative darkness. "I saw him working earlier. Just ask Tom Rockwell. He was here talking to him. Wait. Come to think of it, I saw…" The young man drew in a breath, and his sentence cut out, leaving them hanging as he stared off into the distance.

Lou felt like there was more to that sentence, but before she could ask what he'd seen, an ambulance arrived. The vehicle rounded the fence, bumping through the open field before stopping in front of the deadly display. EMTs rushed out to help Easton as he pulled the body from the tangle of lights.

"There's no way Tom Rockwell was here with Arthur," the purple-scarf-wearing woman scoffed, pulling Lou's attention back to what the young man had just said. "The two of them haven't talked in ages."

"Yeah, not since Arthur cut Tom out of the business," Hayden said.

"Shhh, everyone." Ruby, the manager of the local coffee shop, scuttled over. "Chandler and Elise are standing right over there." She gestured to a couple who looked to be in their forties, huddled together next to the fence as they watched the terrible scene across the field.

"Tom's son and his wife," Willow whispered to Lou and her parents, knowing they wouldn't understand the reason they needed to keep their voices down. "Tom and Arthur used to run A-Plus together, and it's still a sore subject."

Lou recognized Elise. "Oh, she works at the boutique. Right?"

Willow nodded.

"That place looked cute," Caroline said. "I think I'll have to do some shopping tomorrow." She cringed, glancing at the police who were dealing with Arthur's body, embarrassed to have been thinking about shopping at such a time.

Despite Ruby's warning, the group continued their conversation about Arthur and Tom.

Ducking his head and leaning closer to the group, Santa Hat Guy tsked. "Arthur didn't kick him out. Tom decided to leave the business when Penny was diagnosed."

"Whatever the reason, Jill's right. Arthur and Tom haven't talked in ages," Hayden said. "Ferris, are you sure it was Tom you saw?" He turned to look where the younger man in the bright orange sweatshirt had been standing.

But Ferris was gone.

Santa Hat Guy scanned the crowd. "That's weird. Where'd he go?"

Murmurs of discontent moved through the small group.

"This Arthur, do you think he fell while he was working?" Bruce asked, turning to watch the EMTs and police work. Another cruiser had arrived, and officers were using the headlights of the vehicles to cut through the inky blanket of night.

The group of locals regarded Bruce for a moment as if just realizing there was someone new among them.

"These are my parents, everyone," Lou said. "They're visiting me for a month."

They welcomed the couple to town.

"How do you think he died?" Bruce clarified his earlier question, emboldened by being introduced by his daughter.

"Arthur wasn't a spring chicken," Jill, the woman wearing the purple scarf, said. "It's dangerous to get up on those tall ladders in your prime, let alone when you're close to retirement."

"Especially when you're not used to manual labor." Hayden shook his head in disappointment. "I wonder why he was up there in the first place. He has guys who usually do that kind of work."

Ruby snorted. "Yeah, I haven't seen that man lift a finger in years."

Bruce studied the faces of the locals surrounding them. "He was really that bad?"

Hayden widened his eyes. "Really."

"The man pinched his pennies so hard they'd bend in half," Jill explained.

"A real character," the guy in the Santa hat said.

"Someone you wouldn't be surprised to find stealing from little old ladies?" Bruce crossed his arms.

The group nodded approvingly, seeing Bruce in a different light. They stood up straighter, tipping their heads to the side. Even if he wasn't a local, Lou got the feeling that he had their seal of approval. She bit back a smirk. Her didn't just charm five-year-olds. People of all ages were drawn to him, many becoming new friends after only a few minutes of conversation.

Caroline, ever the rational one, stepped forward. "The lights don't seem to be wrapped around his neck, though. How did he die?"

At her question, they all turned back toward the tree line.

"Maybe he had a heart attack while he was up there," Hayden suggested. "He could've gotten tangled up on the way down."

They speculated about a few more possibilities as they huddled close in the cold. There must've been enough police on the scene at that point, because Noah and the others who'd followed Easton at first rejoined the people standing by the fence.

Lou walked over to meet Noah, crossing her arms tight to stave off the icy chill trying to creep into her bones. "Is it really

Arthur Crawford? Is he dead?" she asked as Willow and her parents flanked her, closing in on Noah to hear his report.

Noah's posture was hunched as he said, "It's Arthur, and he's dead all right."

"Did he fall and get tangled?" Bruce asked.

Noah flinched. "That's what it looks like, though nothing's for sure. We can't see much in the dark. He probably got an accidental shock and it was too much for his heart."

A hush fell over the crowd as Easton walked over next.

"Hey, everyone, sorry for the turn of events. You can all go home. Is Chandler Rockwell still around?" Easton scanned the crowd.

A man stepped forward, the same man Ruby had worried would overhear them discussing his father's prior business partnership earlier. His wife stayed put, clutching the chain-link fence as she waited for her husband.

"I'm still here, Easton." Chandler ducked his head a little as he walked forward, like he might be in trouble.

At that, Lou narrowed her eyes. Willow elbowed her to show she found the behavior odd, too but she kept her gaze locked on the middle-aged man as Easton moved toward him.

"Can I ask you to come with me for a second?" Easton motioned for him to follow him.

Chandler followed, and their voices grew distant as Lou lost them in the night. The only sign of their destination was Easton's flashlight, illuminating the gray metal transformer box along the very edge of the field.

A large section of the remaining crowd wandered toward their cars in the parking lot, heading home at Easton's urging. A few groups remained, however, including the one that had gathered around Bruce.

Noah and Lou's father had returned to the clump of locals

they'd been hanging around earlier, and Bruce had them engrossed in a story about a student trying to stick a bent paperclip into one of his classroom power outlets. Lou stepped farther away so she could watch Easton and Chandler as they stopped at the transformer box.

"What do you think he's looking at over there?" Willow whispered, having followed her.

"Do you think Arthur could've been electrocuted like Noah suggested?" Lou asked, jumping to the only conclusion that made sense.

"Chandler still works for A-Plus Electric, so Easton's probably asking his opinion." Willow raised an eyebrow with interest.

"Of course electrocution is a possibility," Caroline said, walking up next to Willow.

Lou and Willow turned their attention to Caroline. After working in construction for her whole career, she knew much more about electrical systems than they did.

Caroline must've gotten the hint that they needed more information because she elaborated as they watched Easton and Chandler walk back to rejoin the group.

"One shock is bad enough, but being wrapped up like he was means he could've been continually shocked until his heart stopped," she explained. "Though, they usually turn off the power when they're working on a line like this."

"Maybe he got lazy," Willow said.

"Yeah." Lou nodded. "The people around us seemed to think Arthur hadn't been in the field in a while. Maybe he forgot to take the proper safety precautions, or didn't think he needed to for a Christmas display."

Easton approached the three women, a grimace creating dark shadows on his face. "I wish that was the case." He kept his voice low so the group Bruce was talking with, off to the right, wouldn't be able to hear.

Chandler rejoined his wife, and they headed toward the parking lot. The only people left were the ones crowded around Lou's father, listening to yet another anecdote.

"You mean it wasn't accidental?" Lou whispered.

Easton's blue eyes seemed almost gray in the dark as he said, "The Christmas lights have been stripped in a few places to expose the wires, and someone removed the safety lock on the transformer box. It was lying in the grass a few feet away."

"What does that mean?" Willow asked, her question hanging in the chilly night air like the threat of a storm.

"It means," Easton said, "that Arthur Crawford was murdered."

CHAPTER 3

Lou and her family didn't stick around the park much longer than that.

Back at the bookshop, Lou hung her jacket on the coatrack by the door. A shiver immediately wriggled up her back. The apartment was warm, proving that the chill Lou was experiencing had more to do with Arthur's death being ruled a murder than just the cold weather.

Lou wasn't the only one shivering; Willow turned on the gas fireplace, standing in front of the direct heat and rubbing her hands up and down her arms. Bruce sank onto the couch, shaking his head.

But Caroline turned on the oven.

"What are you doing, Mom?" Lou asked as her mother opened the refrigerator and pulled out a dozen eggs.

"I'm making cookies." Caroline nodded resolutely, setting down the eggs so she could rifle through the cabinets in search of Lou's flour and sugar.

Willow's eyes lit up. "I'm in." She joined Caroline in the

kitchen, pulling a clean apron from one of the drawers and pointing Caroline toward the mixing bowls.

"Tonight?" Lou asked. "Don't you think it's…" But Lou didn't know how to finish that sentence. It wasn't as if it was too late to bake. And now that Lou thought about it, cookies seemed like the perfect thing to warm up her cold bones after their chilling evening.

"We have to turn the night around." Caroline placed her palms on the countertop. "I won't have my first night in Button end on that note." She huffed. "Therefore, we need to salvage the situation. I'm going to start by making our family sugar cookies."

The sweet cookies with just a hint of lemon and spice were bound to put a smile on anyone's face. But it was more than that. The routine of making the dough, cutting out the various shapes and decorating the cookies together always made Lou feel warm inside and made her feel connected to her family. Even as an adult, whenever they made the family recipe, it gave Lou flashbacks of her childhood Christmases.

Bruce put on some Christmas music and danced around the living room, making them all laugh.

While Caroline made the dough, Lou and Willow prepped the decorating station. Lou had ordered as many sprinkles as she could find to prepare for her parents' arrival, knowing that Christmas cookie making would be on their to-do list. By the time Caroline had the first batch chilling in the refrigerator, Bruce had danced over to help choose that year's cookie cutters. It was a Welsh family tradition to include just as many non-Christmas related shapes as traditional ones. So besides candy canes, Christmas trees, angels, and stars, Lou had a dinosaur, a horse, a dog, and even a cowboy hat.

"I think we definitely have to use this one," Bruce said, holding up the cowboy hat cutter.

Lou giggled. "Whatever you want, Dad."

"Is that really your choice?" Caroline placed a hand on her apron-protected hip.

Bruce studied the metal outline of a cowboy hat for a moment. "Yep. I feel darn sure about it, partner." He set the cookie cutter next to the rolling station.

To balance out Bruce's nontraditional choice, Caroline chose the angel. Willow's choice was, unsurprisingly, the horse. She said the outline looked just like her beloved chestnut gelding, OC.

Lou's fingers hovered indecisively over the stack of leftover cookie cutters, unsure which to pick. Her fingers hovered over the Christmas tree shape. The tree was usually one of her favorites. The large area was great for decorations, and it was nice to have some bigger cookies mixed in with the smaller shapes.

But she hesitated. A Christmas tree seemed a little too sad after what they'd witnessed tonight at the town's Christmas tree lighting.

"Christmas dinosaur, it is," Lou muttered as she reached for the metal tyrannosaurus rex outline, and she made a mental note to find a cat cookie cutter for next year.

An hour later, Willow pulled the last batch of cookies from the oven. They decorated the tray and turned off the oven. Caroline had them cleaned up and all the cookies put into tins in no time at all.

Willow stared in awe at the clean kitchen and stacks of

cookie tins. "Care Bear, you're a force of nature. Lou, don't you think Julia needs someone like Caroline to help with the Christmas production?" Willow asked, her question dripping in complaint.

Caroline's eyes lifted with interest. "Christmas production?"

"Willow's volunteering with the annual production of *A Christmas Carol* that the elementary is putting on," Lou explained to her parents.

Willow exhaled a pent-up breath. "I'm only doing this as a favor to Noah. His daughter, Marigold, is playing Scrooge, and they're doing a northwest theme, so they wanted a lot of potted plants and ferns. I'm supplying the plants mostly, but I've also been helping with the props since Noah's got his hands full with sewing most of the costumes as well."

"That sounds like a lot," Caroline said, a thoughtful lilt to her words.

"Oh, it is. The teacher who normally puts it on is out on maternity leave, so a parent took it on this year. Julia said she directed a play in college, and she's obviously good with kids, since hers is a sweetheart, but she's not great at directing large groups of little ones. They're running all over her. Of course, it probably would be easier for her if she chatted less with the teachers and other parents and did more directing. I'm not much help since I'm used to high schoolers, so the one time I tried to get them to pay attention, I made half of them cry." Willow let out an exasperated sigh. "And Noah's better with animals than large groups of kids."

At this, Bruce perked up. He and Caroline shared a quick glance.

"We could volunteer, if you think we might be helpful," Caroline suggested.

Bruce puffed out his chest. "I'm great at getting kids to listen, especially the little ones, and Caro here will have everyone on a tight schedule within minutes."

The relief in Willow was evident as she blinked and her lips parted. "You two would do that?"

They nodded.

"But you're retired. You should relax and enjoy your vacation." Willow's forehead folded into a frown.

Caroline placed a hand on Willow's. "We're retired, which means we don't *have to* do certain things anymore. That doesn't mean we can't do them for fun."

"Yeah, as much as I thought I wouldn't, I'm missing being around kids." Bruce rubbed the back of his neck.

Caroline clapped her hands together. "Then it's settled. We'll help as much as we can with the play, as long as it doesn't interfere with us getting in all of our holiday traditions with Lou."

Willow cringed. "The rehearsals are all after school." She pulled out her phone. "When are you planning holiday activities? Then I'll know which ones you can or cannot make."

Caroline looked at Lou and then Bruce, excitement leaking from her eager posture. "I think this calls for a calendar."

Lou bit back a smile. "I'll go print one out."

"And I'll find where Lou keeps her colored pens." Bruce headed for the kitchen counter where Lou stored her mail and had a mugful of pens by a notepad for her grocery lists.

Willow, Lou, and Bruce made their way over to the table. Charles Lickens jumped up, supervising them as they worked and pushing two of the pens Bruce had brought over onto the floor.

Using the Button flyer she'd gotten under her door last week, Lou filled in all the Button Christmas events in blue ink.

She included the Christmas tree lighting, even if it hadn't exactly gone to plan.

Willow checked her calendar on her phone, and they wrote each play practice on the calendar in red ink. With those days set aside, they filled in the open days with Welsh family Christmas traditions. Those events were written in green until they had something on almost every day of the December calendar.

"I think the only thing left is wreath making." Caroline tapped the pen on the table.

"Well, it can't go on this day." Lou placed the pen tip in the box for the following Wednesday.

"Why?" Bruce and Caroline asked in unison.

Lou and Willow smiled at each other, excited about what they were about to share.

"We're doing an author event at the bookstore," Lou explained.

"Your first one," Caroline exclaimed proudly.

"And it's a doozy," Willow confirmed.

Bruce cocked an eyebrow in question.

"A few people may have heard of her." Lou held her chin high as she wrote *Olivia Queen Signing* on the calendar.

Caroline drummed her fingers on the table excitedly.

"We finally get to meet the famous Olivia?" Bruce asked in disbelief.

Lou's parents were big fans of Olivia's books, devouring each new release the same week, sometimes even the same day it was published.

"Yep," Lou confirmed. "She called last week. She told her publicist she wanted to stop at Whiskers and Words during her West Coast tour, so she was planning on coming to visit my new shop anyway, but she just found out that her signing right before was canceled, and she'll have a few extra days in town."

Olivia Queen had been one of Lou's clients when she'd been an editor in New York. In fact, Lou's discovery of Olivia's debut novel in the slush pile had been what had promoted Lou from an unpaid intern to an assistant editor, when she'd first started in the publishing business fifteen years earlier. Olivia's insistence on working with Lou, and the fact that her series was a breakaway hit, meant Lou found a place in the publishing house's upper management more quickly than she would have otherwise. And while Lou owed Olivia for that, Olivia maintained that she wouldn't be anywhere without Lou pulling her novel out of the slush pile and insisting her editor read it.

Not only was Lou ecstatic about getting the chance to catch up with Olivia, but she knew it would mean a lot to her parents to have a book signed by one of their favorite authors.

"So then tomorrow's really the only day for wreath making," Lou said, glancing back at the calendar.

"That works for me." Willow nodded. "Some guys at the parks department save the pine boughs they have to cut when they make sure they're not growing into power lines or the roads; they give them out for free around the holidays for people to make wreaths. I can stop by tomorrow afternoon and pick up a bunch."

Caroline beamed. "That sounds perfect." She wrote in the last event, then surveyed the calendar as if it were a work of art. "Even with this busy schedule, it looks like we'll still get to help you out in the bookshop most days too."

DECEMBER

SUN	MON	TUE	WED	THU	FRI	SAT
				1 *Button tree lighting* / *Bake cookies*	2 *Wreath making*	3 *Town Christmas market*
4 *Make family Christmas cards*	5 *Find and decorate Christmas tree*	6 *Play practice*	7 *Olivia Queen Signing*	8 *Play practice* / *Mail Christmas cards*	9 *Button handbell concert*	10 *Button gingerbread house competition*
11 *Button jingle bell run*	12 *Play practice* / *Game night*	13 *Play dress rehearsal* / *Christmas PJs*	14 *Performance: A Christmas Carol*	15 *Christmas movie marathon*	16 *Button Christmas stroll*	17 *Button holiday train rides*
18 *Button High School Madrigal Feast*	19 *Decoration drive around*	20 *Present wrapping*	21 *Town carol singing*	22 *Button holiday food drive*	23	24 *Christmas Eve*
25 *Christmas Day*	26	27	28	29	30	31

Bruce perused the calendar as if he were searching for something specific but didn't see it there. "Any chance there's room to do a little investigating in that schedule?" he asked coyly.

Caroline gave him a gentle slap on the arm. "Bruce, we are not getting involved in that man's murder."

"Why not?" he asked. "Lou's gotten herself entangled in the last few cases in town. You've heard the same stories I have."

It was true that Lou had shared some of her sleuthing adventures with her parents, much after the fact. They had a weekly call on Sunday evenings, but Lou never wanted to worry them, so she only shared about her close calls with villains and murderers well after the danger had passed.

"Mom's right," Lou said to her father. "There's no reason for us to get involved in this investigation. Easton and the police department have it under control, I'm sure."

Bruce squared his shoulders. "I guess you're right. Sounds like a pretty straightforward case of a Scrooge getting what's due to him, after all."

Caroline gasped. "Really, Bruce? That's so crass."

He wrinkled his nose. "I guess no one really deserves *that*. I just hate to see people ignoring the Golden Rule."

"Treat others as you would like to be treated?" Willow guessed.

Bruce winked, showing her she was correct. "It was the backbone of my kindergarten class."

It definitely sounded like Arthur had been treating the locals terribly for decades. Lou was glad she wasn't in Easton's shoes. It seemed like the list of people who might want him dead was as long as their list of holiday activities.

CHAPTER 4

The next day, the bookshop was hopping, even for a Friday. Actually, Lou didn't exactly notice the influx of customers at first, because of her parents.

From the moment Lou flipped the lock on the front door, and switched the sign from Closed to Open, Caroline and Bruce were like a well-oiled machine. It was no surprise that the two fit into Lou's bookshop so well. Lou's parents had raised her on a steady diet of classics and detective novels.

So when Bruce immediately fell into a deep discussion with one of Lou's regulars about the new Stephen King novel, Lou merely smiled. And when Caroline disappeared into the used-book section to organize, Lou knew her mother would have the entire section looking perfect come lunchtime.

Caroline didn't disappoint, unveiling a new, color-coded, organizational system a few hours later. She even managed to take a break to go check out the boutique next door, returning with a bagful of purchases.

Noon rolled around, and Lou couldn't help but think that the bookshop looked better than ever. Between the fire crackling in the fireplace, the cats sleeping in various cozy cat beds around the bookshop, and the light instrumental Christmas music Lou had playing in the background, it felt like the perfect afternoon.

Well, almost perfect.

The problem was that Lou and her parents worked *so* well together, they were bored beyond measure by the second half of the day. So much so that Bruce tried to get rid of Lou so he and Caroline might have more work to do.

"Take advantage of us being here. You don't have to be shackled to this place." Bruce rested his elbows on the counter.

"I'm all right here. I promise," Lou assured her father.

The truth was, she never felt shackled to the bookshop. It was her solace, her dream, and after almost to a year of running it, she never saw it as a burden.

"But you're here all day, every day. Don't you want a break? We can watch the shop for you," Bruce pushed.

Willow blew into the shop with a gust of wind, catching Bruce's last sentence.

"Are you going somewhere?" Willow asked, swiveling to face Lou.

Lou rolled her eyes at her parents. "No. I'm being pressured to leave, though. Why?" The way Willow's posture had tensed, then relaxed upon her hearing that Lou wasn't going anywhere, intrigued her.

"I was wondering if you could do me a favor," Willow admitted.

"Oh, sure," Lou said, the request catching her off guard. Willow rarely asked for favors, especially since Lou was usually the sole proprietor at her bookshop.

"I came to ask Bru and Care Bear, actually, but if they want to stay, it'll be easier for you to do this," Willow said. "I was wondering if you could pick up those pine boughs for our wreath making. I was on my way to do it, but I got a call from Eddie," Willow said, mentioning the man who owned the building next to her nursery, "and it sounds like there might be a leak in one of my watering lines. I have to go handle that now, but Ferris said he's got something going on later and can only meet me this afternoon."

"Sure." Lou checked with her parents to make sure their offer still stood. When they nodded, she added, "I can definitely do that. You said Ferris is holding them?"

"Ferris Howe," Willow confirmed.

Lou was always happy to help out her friend, but it didn't hurt that she was pretty sure that was the same young man who'd disappeared so quickly in the crowd after Arthur's death last night. Lou wouldn't pass up the opportunity to question the man. Only to make sure his story matched with whatever he'd told Easton, of course.

"Where am I meeting him?" Lou asked, grabbing her purse from under the counter.

"At the maintenance building in the park." Willow cringed. "Where we were last night."

"I can do that." Lou gave her a thumbs-up to show it wasn't a big deal. "Good luck with your watering issue."

Clasping her hands together in thanks, Willow said, "You're the best." Then she turned to Bruce and Caroline. "And thank you for watching the place so she can leave."

Lou's parents said it was nothing, waving the two off. Willow headed out the front door, but Lou went out the back, where her car was parked in the alley. Her parents' RV took up a large amount of the space in between her bookshop and the Button Boutique, but there was still room for Lou and someone from the boutique to park near the end of the alley.

The back door to the boutique screeched open as Lou made her way to her car. She recognized the woman, Elise, who'd been huddled next to Chandler Rockwell the night before at the tree lighting. She held a bag of trash, walking it over to their shared dumpster.

"Hi." Lou waved.

Elise tossed the bag into the dumpster and returned the gesture.

"Sorry about this monstrosity." Lou's gaze cut to the RV. "They'll only be here for the month."

"Oh, it's no problem for me." Elise smiled and rubbed her arms against the cold. "Heather told me you cleared it with her beforehand, so you're fine."

"Thanks. I'll see you around." Lou climbed into her car to head to Button Memorial Park for the second time in so many days.

It was odd to see the park during the daylight. Yellow police tape still hung, cordoning off the area by the tree-lighting ceremony. The intact lights looked like skeletons hanging in the trees, while the section Arthur had been caught up in had been removed, no doubt taken by the police as evidence, especially if the section had been stripped to expose the metal like Easton had said last night.

A screeching of tires made Lou jump as she got out of her car. She turned to see a black truck speeding away, out of the parking lot. Smoke billowed out of the tailpipe.

"Someone's in a hurry." Lou clicked her tongue.

Other than the black truck and another pickup with a much older, rustier paint job, Lou's car was the only one in the lot. It wasn't a surprise since it was just after lunch on a Friday.

Lou spotted the maintenance building and walked in that direction.

"Hello," she called out as she stopped under the large metal garage door that had been raised about halfway. Hearing nothing, she walked inside.

A large stack of pine boughs sat on a workbench in the corner. "Ferris," she called, searching around the small maintenance building. "I'm here to pick up the pine boughs you're holding for Willow Grey." Her fingers lingered on the rough workbench as she listened for any signs of the man.

She was about to give up, grab the boughs, and take off when she spotted a pair of men's boots peeking out from behind the door of the storeroom in the back corner of the building. A chill washed over her skin. Unless Ferris had decided to take a nap on the concrete floor of the maintenance building office, things weren't looking good for the young man.

Slipping her phone out of her pocket, she dialed Easton's number as she crept forward. The ringing sound in her ear seemed to get louder as she tiptoed into the office. Ferris, the same young man she had seen at the Christmas tree lighting last night, lay unmoving on the floor.

An orange extension cord was wrapped around his throat.

"Hey, Lou. What's up?" Easton answered. His tone was rushed as if he were busy. Given that the phone had rung for quite a while before he'd picked up, Lou figured he was swamped with Arthur's murder.

And she was about to give him something else to worry about.

"Ferris Howe is dead," she croaked out the words, her esophagus feeling icy and brittle. Lou knelt next to the body, using the tips of her fingers to steady herself on the cold concrete floor.

"What?" Easton spat out the question.

Lou reached as far forward as she dared, letting her fingertips settle on the inside of the man's wrist. She gulped as she felt nothing, only skin that was rapidly cooling. "He's here at the maintenance building at Button Memorial. I came to grab some pine boughs for Christmas wreaths, and he's here with an extension cord wrapped around his neck. I think someone strangled him."

The rustling of papers in the background told Lou that Easton was literally dropping what he'd been working on. "I'll be right there," he said. "Do you want me to stay on the line with you while you wait?"

She appreciated his kindness. "I'm okay. But I might wait outside."

"Understandable." He let out a dry laugh. "I'll be right there."

Lou hung up, getting to her feet. She needed to get away from Ferris's blank stare. Edging out of the small office, Lou waited outside, wrapping her arms around herself, and tucking her gloveless hands under her arms to keep warm in the frosty air.

She tried to move a few steps away from the building, but the transformer box someone had utilized to electrocute Arthur stood right in front of her. So she walked in the other direction, toward the parking lot.

A metal fence ran the length of the field, closing it off from the parking lot, save for two openings. They were the kind of openings where a small piece of fence was placed about two feet from the rest of the fence so people had to weave around and through in order to leave. Lou had seen plenty of these in New York City, made to discourage people from bringing bikes or other large pieces of equipment onto the field.

But there was something different about this one. On the right side of the opening in the fence, there was a magnet stuck to the metal. It was about the size of a pat of butter, and it took a little coaxing, but Lou pried it from the fence and turned it over as she studied it.

Her concentration on the magnet broke when Easton's car pulled up, followed by two Button Police Department cruisers. He barked out orders in such a quick and focused manner, Lou expected him to speak to her at the same volume when he approached. She stuck the magnet back to the fence and walked forward.

"Hey," he said, his voice soft. "I'm going inside to check things out before I take your statement. Do you mind waiting?"

Lou shook her head.

"Do you want to sit in your car so you can stay warm?" he suggested.

Lou was about to turn down the offer when she realized she couldn't really feel her fingertips. She hadn't brought gloves or the correct jacket for standing out in the cold for long periods of time.

"That would be nice." Lou stuffed her hands into her pockets and went to go start her car and sit with the heat on while Easton disappeared into the building, following his officers.

About ten minutes later, Easton emerged from the building, walking over to Lou's car. He slid into the passenger seat. "Sorry you had to see that."

Lou's gaze flicked over to him. "Do you think it was Arthur's killer? Were they trying to shut him up so he couldn't tell you what he saw?"

"Why would you say that?" Easton asked.

Lou explained what she, and many of the townspeople, had heard him say about having seen Tom Rockwell talking to Arthur before he died. "And then he said, 'Wait. Come to think of it, I saw…' and was gone before we could get him to finish. It sounded to me like he'd seen something."

"And if you thought that, the killer could've overheard it as well." Easton rubbed at his chin. "The sad part is, he knew nothing."

"What?" Lou whirled to face Easton.

"Nothing new, that is. He came and talked to us this morning." Easton's tone dropped with sadness. "We already knew about Tom Rockwell and Arthur talking that afternoon."

"That was it?" Lou blinked, recalibrating to this new understanding. "There seemed to be more to it than that."

"Right. Which still helps us. It means the killer might have been in the crowd last night," Easton reasoned. "If they heard him say what you heard, and came to the same conclusion, they would definitely have cause to get him out of the picture."

"But why wait to kill him until he'd already talked to you?" Lou frowned. None of it made sense.

Easton's phone rang, and he answered the call. "Hey, Brenner. Did you find anything?"

While Lou had no intention of listening in on his conversation, she was only sitting a couple of feet away, and Officer Brenner was a loud talker. She couldn't hear everything, but she definitely caught that Brenner was with a team searching Ferris's apartment. The words "blackmail letter" spilled out of the phone, catching her ear.

"Interesting. Well, that clears a few things up. Thank you, and keep me posted if you find anything else." Easton ended the call. He hesitantly turned to look at Lou. "How much of that did you hear?"

She pressed her lips together and wrinkled her nose.

Easton sighed. "So you know why he changed his story."

"He didn't tell you the whole truth," Lou said. "He must've

realized he had to come in and tell you *something* since a bunch of us at the lighting heard him bragging about what he'd seen, but he also must've realized that he could make some money with the extra information he held," Lou said.

Easton nodded. "Brenner said the blackmail letter in his trash had a few things crossed out, so it looks like it was his first draft. There could still be a chance that he changed his mind about the blackmail, which means we're looking for someone who was at the event last night and overheard him. But I'd say it's even more likely that he sent the final copy of the blackmail letter to someone and that person decided to take him out of the picture instead of paying."

"It definitely helps narrow down the killer since they'll have to have two alibis now," Lou pointed out.

"You know we don't need any help, right?" Easton shot her a sidelong glance.

"Me? I was just thinking aloud." She touched her fingers to her collarbone.

Easton sighed. "Sure, but—"

"Did my dad say something to you?" Lou asked.

He shook his head.

"Good." Lou rolled her eyes. "He's got this whole idea that we need to help with the investigation."

Easton chuckled. "Like father, like daughter."

"Don't worry," she said. "I told him we're leaving this one to the professionals."

"Thank you." Easton glanced at his watch. "Now, do you want me to break the news to Willow that she's going to have to wait for those pine boughs until we clear this as a crime scene, or do you want to take the short straw?"

Lou considered the crime scene. "I'm pretty sure you've had enough short straws this week. I'll tell her."

"Thank you." Easton waved as he got out of the car, walking back to the crime scene.

Lou headed back to her bookshop. She called Willow on the way.

"Hey, everything go okay with the pick-up?" Willow asked.

"Um…" Lou pinched the bridge of her nose. "Not exactly. We're going to have to find another place to get pine boughs."

Willow sucked in a surprised breath.

Lou continued, knowing the statement would need elaboration. "The ones Ferris was holding for us are now part of a crime scene. Ferris Howe is dead. He saw something last night that got him killed."

CHAPTER 5

By the time Lou parked in the alley behind the bookstore once more, her shoulders dragged, and fatigue overcame her. She wasn't worried about not having the pine boughs for their wreath making. More than anything, she was cold and hungry and just needed something to cheer her up.

Her unspoken wishes were granted as she walked into the bookshop. While seeing cats inside was never a surprise, she had to do a double take as she saw at least ten kittens rushing around a small pen set up in the middle of the space.

Noah stood next to it, talking to Lou's parents.

Caroline looked up, her cheeks rosy with a wide smile. "We figured out how to make sure we're not bored!"

Noah stepped forward, worry creasing his forehead. "You do not have to take all of them, or any of them. I just figured you'd want to meet them."

Lou couldn't help but chuckle, glancing down at the adorable little balls of fluff. There were white ones, tortoiseshell ones, orange ones, and gray ones. Some had long, fluffy fur, and others were sleek.

"How many of them are there?" she asked, unable to count when they were bounding around, playing with one another.

"Twelve," Noah said with a cringe. When Lou looked at him in wide-eyed question, he added, "Two separate litters, born three days apart to two clients, but I convinced them to let the kittens stay with the mothers for thirteen weeks. Because they listened to me, I told them I'd be happy to help them find suitable homes."

Lou puffed out her cheeks. "Twelve is really going to put a dent in my literary names list."

"Not if your father has anything to say about it," Caroline said as she scooped up a little white kitten. She gestured over to Bruce, who was holding two kittens at once.

"There's twelve of them, and it's December," Bruce said, as if that was enough of an explanation.

For his daughter, it was. "The Twelve Days of Christmas." Nostalgia swirled through Lou like sparkling snow as she thought about the popular song.

A huge grin peeled across Bruce's face and he set down the kittens. He started ticking off the names on his fingers. "I figure we've got Partridge, Turtle, Frenchie, Birdie, Goldie, Goose, Swan, Milky, Lady, Lord, Piper, and Drumstick." Having used some of his fingers twice as he was counting off the names, Bruce wiggled them like it didn't really matter.

"I can see where you get your talent for naming cats." Noah appraised Bruce, obviously impressed.

Lou surveyed the kittens, then looked back at Noah. "Well, it looks like we'll take them all."

He smiled. "Are you sure? You really don't have to, even with the cute names."

"Nonsense," Caroline said, setting down the white kitten she held so she could wave a hand at Noah. "The three of us were going crazy enough in here today that we had to kick Lou out so we would have something to do. And that was only our first day. We're here for the month. Taking care of this little army of kittens will be good for us."

"Kick you out?" Noah asked with a chuckle.

Lou couldn't help but bow her head in sadness as she remembered how her errand had ended. "I was supposed to pick up pine boughs from Ferris so we could make wreaths tonight."

"It's really cool that he and the maintenance guys are doing that," Noah said. "Marigold's class got a batch last week for an ornament project. She said the classroom smelled amazing all day."

Even though Noah hadn't caught on to the fact that Lou was without pine boughs, her mother was like a hawk. She appraised Lou, then checked behind her by the door as if she might've dropped her supply as she'd come inside.

"Supposed to?" Caroline asked. "What happened?"

Lou shifted her weight. "Ferris was dead when I got there."

Caroline inhaled, her hand flying to cover her mouth. Her fingers trembled as they hung there for a moment, but then her hands wrapped around Lou's arm as she pulled her daughter over to the seating area in the bookshop. Bruce followed.

Lou hadn't realized how much she needed to sit down until her mother tugged her onto the cushy love seat next to her. She almost closed her eyes as the comfort of the space wrapped around her: just what she needed after a harrowing afternoon.

In addition to the support and comfort she felt emitting from her parents, Lou noticed that another hand lay on her arm. Noah knelt next to her, worry marring his usually calm expression.

"Tell us everything," Caroline said, then added, "if you don't mind."

Lou shook her head. "I don't mind. It's just ... awful." She swallowed.

The front door opened, and two elderly ladies entered. Their eyes, which had already been alight with the prospect of a bookstore and the cute holiday displays Lou had created in the front windows, grew even bigger as they caught sight of the kittens in the pen next to the register. They both let out high-pitched noises that made the kittens stop what they were doing to gawk at the women.

Bruce patted Lou's leg, shooting her a wink. "I've got this, loves. You stay here and chat."

So Lou told them everything. She kept her voice down so she wouldn't possibly scare her customers, but from the oohing and awwing they were doing over the kittens, Lou doubted they could hear anything. Bruce charmed the women almost as much as the kittens did. After telling the customers the names he'd come up with for the kittens, he took them on a tour of the bookshop, showing off all of Lou's thoughtful touches, both holiday related and everyday.

Throughout her story, Lou could hear the women let out heartfelt aww's as they listened to Bruce brag about his daughter.

"There was an extension cord wrapped around his neck," Lou whispered to her mom and Noah as she finished with her recounting of the terrible events from earlier.

Caroline wrapped an arm around Lou and squeezed tight. "Oh, honey. That sounds awful. I'm so sorry."

Noah placed his hand over Lou's and patted it. "Poor Ferris."

"I think he knew who killed Arthur." Lou left it at that, not wanting to spread the clue she'd overheard about the blackmail note.

Caroline snapped her fingers. "Wasn't he the one who'd seen the dead man talking to someone surprising earlier that day?"

"Tom Rockwell," Lou confirmed, picking a piece of lint off the arm of the couch. "But when he said that, the locals started arguing about how Tom wouldn't be caught dead talking to Arthur since they're mortal enemies."

Noah's knees must've been aching from kneeling for so long, because he winced and moved to the chair next to the love seat. "They said they were mortal enemies?" He wrinkled his nose in confusion.

"They're not?" Caroline asked, intrigue written in the way she scooted to the edge of the couch cushion she occupied.

Noah dipped his head from right to left. "I mean, they weren't friends, but I guess I never thought of them as enemies."

"So Arthur didn't kick him out of the business?" Lou asked, glad to have the opinion of a local she could trust. Noah wasn't someone who spread gossip or hearsay.

"Not exactly," Noah explained. "Tom's wife, Penny, got really sick about ten years ago. Tom and Arthur were co-owners of A-Plus Electric back then. Tom was the one who left the company. After Penny's diagnosis, he knew they wouldn't have very much time, and he wanted to spend his energy on her, so he left the company."

"So there were no hard feelings between them?" Lou asked.

Noah squinted one eye. "I can't promise that. Arthur was a

pretty heartless person, so I can't say he handled it with any grace or sympathy. But that's all I know."

"But according to Ferris, he was talking to Arthur earlier in the day, the same day he showed up dead, tangled up in the Christmas lights." Lou tapped her fingers on her lips as she thought through the implications of the information. "And Easton said, not only had someone exposed the wires in multiple places along the string of lights that Arthur had gotten caught up in, but that they had removed the lock on the transformer box, which I'm guessing was there for safety reasons." At this, Lou looked at her mother for confirmation.

Caroline nodded. "Electricians use a lockout/tagout system to make sure there's no one else working on a line before they turn on the power and hurt someone. If Arthur had locked out that box, and someone removed the lock, it means they were trying to hurt him on purpose." Caroline paused.

"What?" Lou asked, wondering about her mother's hesitation.

"It's just ... the locks for the lockout system all have individual keys," Caroline explained. "But sometimes companies will save money by purchasing locks that all open with the same key. That way if one of their workers loses one, they don't have to buy another lockset."

"So we're looking for a killer who's part of A-Plus Electric," Lou inferred, stroking Charles Lickens after he jumped in her lap.

"Or a former employee," Noah said. "Which doesn't look good for Tom."

"Wait a minute. What's going on here?" Bruce stood in front of them, arms crossed.

Lou had gotten so into their discussion, she hadn't even

noticed that the customers had gone, and Bruce was now free to rejoin the conversation.

"I thought we weren't getting involved in the investigation." Bruce glared accusingly at Caroline, since she was the one who had told him to stay out of it. Next, he turned his ire toward his daughter.

Caroline put a hand on Lou's defensively. "We aren't. Lou was just telling us what she saw."

All of Bruce's attitude left him in an instant. "Oh, I'm so sorry, Lou-Lou." He knelt next to his daughter. "I'll make your mother retell it to me if you don't want to go over it again."

"Thanks." She gave him a wan smile, turning to her mother. "I think I'll make myself some tea while you two fill him in."

Noah stood, checking his watch. "I need to get back to the clinic, actually, if Caroline doesn't mind being the reporter. Call me anytime if you need something for the little ones." He motioned over to the pen full of kittens. "I already told Caro and Bruce, but they're all up on their vaccinations. They've also been spayed and neutered, though they need to heal, so it'll be best if they can stay in that pen as long as possible. I'll bring by their paperwork tomorrow."

Lou and her parents said they would see him tomorrow, and waved goodbye to Noah as he headed out into the wintry day. Lou went to the back to make some tea to calm her nerves, but her fingers shook.

Not only was there a murderer in Button, but it didn't seem like they were done killing. And if what Ferris saw had gotten him killed, the biggest question in Lou's mind was, who might be next?

CHAPTER 6

After making herself some tea in the back office of Whiskers and Words, Lou rejoined her parents in the bookshop. Her fingers had stopped shaking and she was feeling warm again after her chilling afternoon.

Lou kept her hands wrapped around the mug. "Sorry to make you doubt my commitment to staying out of things, Dad, but I think this is something best left to Easton and the Button police."

"Your mother and I agree," Bruce said, studying his daughter with the eyes of a worried father. "Don't worry, I'll let it drop."

Lou was the only one in the shop when Willow showed up at closing time with bags full of wreath-making supplies. Caroline was already upstairs getting ready for the craft, and Bruce had wanted to check out Smitty's antique shop.

Before Lou could lock the door behind her friend, Willow pulled her into a piney-smelling hug.

"I'm so sorry," Willow said, her words muffled by her jacket as the hug pushed it up in front of her face. She stepped back, pulling her coat down. "It was supposed to be me." Her face was the picture of distraught apology. "I sent you, and you found him ... dead."

Lou placed a hand on Willow's arm, hoping to erase that terrible look from her friend's features forever. "You couldn't have known. I'm okay. Plus, I've seen more dead bodies than you have, at this point." She tried to make light of it but wasn't sure jokes and talk of murder belonged in the same sentence.

Willow nodded, accepting her friend's insistence that she was okay. "Without the boughs from Ferris, I did as well as I could with the trees on the edge of my property, but they're pretty tall, and I got a little scared up on the ladder in that lumpy field." Willow held up a bag with a bunch of pine boughs protruding from the top. "I also left a message for Peggy Lee, seeing if she could bring anything out, but she might not get here in time."

Peggy Lee was the woman who owned the farm where Willow would source her plants for her nursery when she opened in the spring. She lived about twenty minutes north of Button and had grown close to Willow during the last few months.

"We'll make do with what we have if she doesn't. These look great," Lou assured her.

She was about to go upstairs when Willow stopped short and gasped. "What is this?" She was staring at the pen of sleeping kittens. One or two of them blinked sleepy eyes at her, but they didn't move, which was amazing because it felt like they'd been playing all day long.

Lou bounced on the balls of her feet. "Two different litters. Twelve kittens in all. They're about thirteen weeks old, Noah says, and Dad has named them after the 'Twelve Days of Christmas' song." She giggled before recounting the names to Willow. "Come on upstairs. Mom is getting things ready for us." Lou waved her friend toward the back staircase.

"Bruce isn't joining?" Willow asked, surprised. "He's usually the most into crafts out of all of us."

"He'll join us in a bit," Lou said. "He just wanted to check out Smitty's place after all the bragging I did about the antiques he carries. Dad said it's better that he's not there to ruin Mom's organizing, anyway."

Upstairs, the sight that met them in the apartment was just that. Organized. Caroline had the wires, wreath frames, sprigs of sparkling accents, and dried holly berries separated into neat piles. She'd even set up stations around the table for each of them to work.

"Oh, good." Caroline clasped her hands together as Lou and Willow entered. She reached out for the bag of greenery Willow had brought and immediately made a place for that as well. "Is your father back yet?"

"Not yet. I know Smitty, they're probably chatting away about some obscure collection he has."

A hint of worry flashed over Caroline's features.

"Don't worry," Willow chimed in. "Smitty closes in a few minutes. Bruce will be here soon, I'm sure."

Lou kept it to herself that Smitty stayed open late all the time, especially if he got to talking to a customer.

While they waited for Bruce and chatted, Lou noticed that her best friend's body language was as tight as the green wire she kept fiddling with at her wreath-making station, a sure sign that something was on her mind.

"Okay, Willow. What's going on?" Lou placed a hand on the table. "Honest three."

At the phrase, Caroline placed her hand over her heart. "I just love that you girls still do that. I remember when you came up with it. What was that? Middle school?"

Lou and Willow had been using the prompt for decades to do emotional check-ins with each other. They found that often when they tried to explain how they were doing, it was too easy to sugarcoat authentic emotions or hide how they were really feeling. The rules of honest three were that they had to answer immediately, without overthinking their three words, and there was no judgment cast on the emotions they named.

Willow's tight mouth relaxed, even pulling up into a half smile. "I think we came up with it in high school." She turned to Lou. "Fretting, second-guessing, and driving myself crazy." She let out a self-deprecating laugh.

Caroline took the seat next to Willow at the table. "Oh, honey. Tell us what's going on."

Branches and boughs covered the tabletop, so Willow couldn't slump forward, like it looked like she wanted to, so she leaned back into her seat. "It's Christmas. And it's Easton," she said.

"Separately or together?" Lou asked, pulling out a chair and taking a seat herself. She hoped Willow and Easton weren't having issues. They'd seemed so happy lately.

"Together," Willow said. She turned to Caroline to give her a little background. "We've been on a lot of dates, but I'm not sure if we're in a *relationship* or not. And because I'm not sure where we stand. I don't know what to get him for Christmas. I've been driving myself crazy thinking about it." She groaned. "Like, what if I don't get him anything, but he gets me something? Or vice versa. If I get him a gift, what if one of us gets something way nicer than the other?" She trained her eyes on Lou and then Caroline. "If we'd been dating longer, I don't think this would be such a conundrum. As it is, I feel lost."

Willow wasn't one to care so much about gifts or symbols of a relationship. Which meant that all the nursery prep was getting to her more than she let on. She must be stressed from the constant decision-making she'd been doing for her business, not to mention the fires she'd been putting out, like the leak earlier. Lou could empathize. Opening the bookshop hadn't been easy, either, and it had basically been ready to open compared to the prep work Willow was having to put into the nursery.

Lou put a hand on Willow's arm. "You've been putting in a lot of work at the nursery and now with the play. I don't think Easton would blame you for not putting a ton of effort into a gift."

"Why don't you just ask him what he wants?" Caroline suggested.

Willow let her arms fall into her lap in exasperation. "That's the thing. I already did, and he shrugged and said whatever you want to do."

"Maybe it's not super important to him." Lou sat straighter, hoping this was the answer.

"What's not important to who?" Peggy Lee, Willow's business partner, asked as she walked inside. She glanced down at the bookshop. "Also, did you know that you left the door unlocked downstairs and there's close to twenty kittens downstairs?"

Lou stood. The door. She'd been too distracted to lock it when Willow had arrived.

"Don't worry. I locked it behind me." Peggy Lee motioned

for Lou to relax. "It's cold out there and getting dark, so no one's on the streets. Now tell me more about those kittens."

Lou settled back into her seat, knowing her father had a key so the locked door wouldn't stop him. "The kittens are all up for adoption," she explained to Peggy Lee. "Aren't they great? We thought about bringing them up here at first, but I had visions of them trying to steal our supplies and chewing on everything, so I'm keeping them down there until we finish."

The adult cats from the bookshop were upstairs, however, and they were all perched on the back of the couch, eyes wide as they stalked the branches.

"I'm about to banish these four as well," Lou said, sending a serious look toward the gang of adult cats looking at the supplies on the table as if they might pounce at any moment. She pointed to the fourth seat. "We're glad you could make it, Peggy Lee. This is my mom, Caroline. Have a seat."

Peggy Lee shook Caroline's hand and then pulled some squiggly sticks and fir boughs out of a bag she'd brought with her. "Found a few things on the farm that might be good for this."

Once Caroline had them organized into piles, Peggy Lee sank into the fourth seat around the table. "So ... back to something not being important to someone." Peggy Lee's sharp gaze snapped from Lou to Willow, holding it there as if she knew the issue had to do with Willow.

"I don't know if I should get a gift for Easton," Willow explained, punctuating the sentence with a tired exhale before she went into explaining the subtleties of the predicament to Peggy Lee.

The older woman listened as if Willow were describing how to knit a sweater for a chicken: confused and incredulous. At the end of Willow's description, Peggy Lee snorted and said,

"What's the problem? If he said you can do whatever you want, take him at his word."

Willow stared down at her hands. Lou wrinkled her nose, knowing it wasn't that easy. Even Caroline tilted her head and grimaced.

"What?" Peggy Lee asked, unsure of what was wrong with her statement.

Lou scratched at her cheek while she thought of how to word her response. "Because they haven't had a talk about what kind of relationship they have, or want to have, he might've said that so she doesn't feel pressure."

"Or because he doesn't want a gift from me because that would be too much pressure on him," Willow added.

Peggy Lee shook her head. "That's the most complicated thing I've ever heard. Thank goodness I got to be with the same man for forty years. These new dating rules are confusing."

Lou brightened at Peggy Lee's mention of her late husband. She and the ornery woman had connected over their widow-hood, and Lou had found the woman to be not only softer-hearted than she first thought, but an astute judge of character.

"Maybe Peggy Lee's right." Lou tapped her fingers on her leg. Anne Mice took it as an invitation and rushed over to bat at her hand. She gently pushed the cat away. "What if you just tell him exactly what you're worried about? No games. Just the truth."

Caroline and Peggy Lee said they agreed, but Willow cut the air with her hand.

"Even if I wanted to, the man's busier than Santa right now with two murder investigations on his plate." Willow groaned. "He was going to hand one over to Roy," Willow explained, mentioning the other detective in town, "but the chief said since they're connected, that he should stay the lead on both. He can use Roy as backup if he needs."

"I'm sure Roy would love that," Lou said sarcastically, rolling her eyes.

Detective Roy Anderson was not a fan of hers and remained a bit of a sore subject for Lou ever since he'd suspected her in a local murder.

"Wait. Murders? Plural? What happened?" Peggy Lee peered around the table as she searched for answers.

Caroline calmly filled her in on the two bodies that had been found over the past two days.

"So ... are you going to solve this one too?" Peggy Lee eyed Lou, knowing she was the one who'd cracked the last case.

"I'm afraid not," Lou said. "My good friend Olivia is coming tomorrow, and I want to make sure I'm focused on my first book signing in the shop. Plus, you saw how many kittens are down there."

Peggy Lee held her breath for a second. "I hear you. I've got my hands full with my one."

Her cat, Holden Clawfield, had been with Lou for a few days back before Peggy Lee had adopted him. He was a beautiful flame-point Siamese, but he'd craved being outside in a way Lou just couldn't manage with the bookshop.

"How is he doing with the cold weather?" Lou asked.

Peggy Lee sniffed. "Fine."

"She knit him a little sweater. It's adorable." Willow sent a teasing smirk toward her business partner.

"I—it's—he was—" Peggy Lee stammered, her cheeks turning red.

Lou's heart warmed, and the apartment door opened. Bruce entered with a cloth shopping bag hanging from his arm.

After they introduced him to Peggy Lee, Caroline cocked an eyebrow and motioned to the bag. "What'd you find?"

Bruce's eyes glinted like the Christmas lights strung throughout downtown. He peered inside the bag and began pulling out Christmas ornaments, setting them on the table in what little space remained between the wreath-making supplies.

"I found the coolest vintage ornaments," he explained. "I figured we could add them to the tree this year."

After inspecting the ornaments and assuring Bruce they were a great find, they put them away and got started on their wreath making. Caroline had watched a video in preparation, but Bruce knew a few tips and tricks, having run a few wreath-making classes at his school during the holiday bazaar each year. And if Lou thought the place smelled good before, it was nothing compared to the rich, piney scent that permeated her apartment once they started trimming sprigs and securing them onto the forms.

The conversation was easy and flowing as they worked. Lou sat back and admired the scene around the table. Wreath making was a tradition Ben had started. Lou steadied herself through the familiar pang of loss at the memory of him and let the warmth that followed envelop her.

Not only was her family in town, which gave her a grounded feeling that rivaled being covered by even the coziest blanket, but her chosen family was expanding by the month here in Button. She could feel Ben watching out for her, making sure things went well for her in his absence. And even though this wasn't her first Christmas without him, it still stung, knowing he wouldn't be by her side.

Sure, they had plans to go caroling, but Ben wouldn't be there to sing in a ridiculously low baritone the whole time.

Christmas dinner would be yet again without his famous hot crab fondue, which Lou had tried to recreate last year but couldn't get just right.

Even so, she would be okay. She would create new traditions and was showing herself that she could keep others alive.

A shiver washed over her skin as she glanced outside at the icy street and remembered the deaths piling up in her beloved town. She just hoped finding bodies and trying to unearth a killer wouldn't become a holiday tradition too.

CHAPTER 7

Lou got so many compliments on her wreath the next day that she almost didn't even look up from her computer when a woman said, "What a lovely wreath you have hanging out front."

Except ... that voice.

"Olivia!" Lou raced around the checkout counter toward the woman who had been such a big part of her previous career.

Olivia Queen was a few inches taller than Lou. The slight hunch in her shoulders, and the gray hairs peeking through her dark brown hair were the only signs Lou could see that put her close to Caroline's and Bruce's ages. She lived in the color black and she always had her worn laptop bag hanging off one shoulder.

Olivia walked forward to meet Lou. "It's so good to see you, sweetie." She wrapped her arms around Lou and squeezed tight. Even though she'd been a New York City cop for decades, and could be a little blunt, the woman was also one of the kindest, most thoughtful people Lou knew, and usually called her sweetie.

She wore thin-wired glasses that perched on her nose, and Lou knew there would be at least three more pairs stuffed in her large purse. She also knew there would be a laptop and at least one book inside the satchel that hung from Olivia's thin shoulder.

As the two women let go of each other and stepped back, Lou realized her parents were standing about ten feet behind Olivia, exuding excitement. They were obviously trying to give the friends space, while still being as close as they dared. Caroline's shoulders pulled up in anticipation, and Bruce lifted his graying eyebrows.

Lou bit at her lip to hide her amusement. "Olivia, these are my parents, Caroline and Bruce Welsh."

Olivia spun around. "I was so thrilled when Lou mentioned that you two were visiting for the month and that I would finally get to meet you." As she talked, she walked over, pulling each of them into a hug.

Lou's parents were huggers, thankfully, so neither was taken aback by the gesture.

"*You're* thrilled?" Bruce choked out the words.

Lou had rarely seen her charismatic father anything close to speechless. She was suddenly glad there weren't any customers in the bookshop just then, sure her father wouldn't be the only one starstruck.

"We're such big fans," Caroline supplied when Bruce didn't provide anything more than the stuttered question. "Not only of your friendship and business relationship with our daughter but also of your books. Your last one was so perfect."

The smile on Olivia's face was genuine but a little tight. Lou knew the woman had a hard time taking praise or having the full spotlight on her. She was getting better, and often had no issue when it was a signing or an event with complete strangers, but she still seemed stiff and uncomfortable around friends and family when someone brought up her books.

"Thank you so much. I'm happy to hear that. I think I'm hitting my stride with this new editor." She winked at Lou. "My first manuscript without Lou was a learning curve, for sure, but I think we're finding our rhythm."

"Lori is a wonderful editor. She did a great job with both of your latest books," Lou said.

Caroline and Bruce nodded emphatically.

"You know, this lady offered to keep remotely editing my books for me," Olivia said, hooking a thumb toward Lou.

Appreciation tugged the corners of Lou's mouth into a grin. "This latest one," she clarified. "I couldn't have done the one before that."

Any happiness she'd been experiencing slipped away as she remembered Olivia had turned in a manuscript right around the time Ben died. Lou had been a mess and could barely get dressed in the morning, let alone do her job.

"But you turned her down," Bruce said matter-of-factly, having recovered his ability to speak in the presence of a celebrity. He understood why Olivia had refused Lou's offer and obviously liked her even more for it.

"Lou needed this new life." Olivia shot an endearing look at Lou. "She didn't need ties to her old one any more than she needed an anchor pulling her to the bottom of the ocean."

Caroline hummed in agreement, smiling over at her daughter.

"As much as I would've loved to have had Lou edit my books for the rest of my life, I knew she needed a fresh start." Olivia surveyed the bookshop as if seeing it for the very first time, even though she'd been standing inside it for almost five minutes at that point. "And look at it. What a fresh start it's been for you, sweetie. I'm so proud of you."

Tears crowded Lou's eyes for just a moment at the warmth and truth she felt surrounding the statement, but she blinked them away.

"It really has been wonderful here. I can't wait to show you around town," Lou said.

"Oh, and for you to meet Willow." Caroline clasped her hands to her chest.

Olivia's eyes shone. "Willow and I have met, actually, but I can't wait to spend more time with her."

At this, Caroline sent a questioning glance at Lou.

"One of Willow's visits to New York City coincided with an event we were doing with Olivia, and they hit it off." Lou smiled at the memory.

"But I'd like to get to know you two better," Olivia said, reaching forward to grab Caroline's hands affectionately. "And the cats!" Olivia placed her palms on her cheeks as she took in the four adult cats lounging throughout the bookshop and the dozen tumbling around during playtime in the kitten pen. "I didn't picture there would be so many. Hello, Sapphy," she added, scratching the white cat's head as she walked by him toward the kitten pen.

"There weren't until yesterday," Lou explained.

"Lou's friends with the local veterinarian, and two of his clients had litters a couple of days apart," Caroline explained.

"Noah's the one who works with me on the adoptions," Lou said.

"A solid guy," Bruce added with a fatherly nod of approval.

"He's a bit of a jack-of-all-trades around here," Lou

explained. "He's the local vet, but he also takes on odd jobs as a handyman, and his family owns the quilting shop down the street, so he helps there when he can."

As she described Noah's penchant for keeping busy, Lou wondered if he'd always had that many things going on at once, or if he'd adopted so many hobbies after his divorce to keep his mind occupied.

Lou snapped out of her thought process, realizing that her father was pointing out the kittens to Olivia and telling her their names.

"The three tortoiseshells are Turtle, Piper, and Drumstick," Bruce said. "The only orange one is Goldie." He turned to Olivia. "Noah told us that most orange cats are males, so the fact that she's a female is rare. We thought Goldie fit just right."

Lou loved seeing how much her father was enjoying the kittens.

"Now, let's see ... there are three tabbies, that all look alike, so I've gotta go by their collars." He squinted down at the playful kittens. "Yes, the one with the green collar is Partridge. Frenchie has the purple collar, and Birdie is in the pink there. Lady is that all-black one in the middle. Lord is black with four white paws, but Goose is all black with the little white mustache, like mine," Bruce said, beaming at the last kitten for a second longer than the others. "And the two white ones are Swan and Milky." He clapped his hands together to punctuate the end of the introductions, causing the kittens to skitter to the other side of the pen in surprise. "Oh, sorry, little ones." Bruce leaned down to coax them back over so he could apologize.

Lou didn't miss the way her father had paused after talking about Goose. She also hadn't missed how he seemed to hold that kitten more than all the others.

After a few minutes of cooing over the kittens—and saying hello to the older cats too—Olivia turned her attention to Bruce and Caroline and said, "It really is so great to meet the two of you."

Caroline led her over to the seating area where they plopped into the comfy cushions of the couch, and Bruce took a seat in the chair opposite. A group of women wandered in the shop, perusing the new-release display toward the front door.

"I'm going to hang out over here and help customers," Lou called.

From the seating area, she heard Olivia ask, "So I hear you just retired. How's that been going? Where have you traveled so far?"

Olivia only had a slight New York accent, having moved to the city when she was in her early twenties, much like Lou. Her familiar voice wafted through the shop as Lou assisted the group of women, who bought a few Regency romance titles. Lou couldn't help but be filled with happiness at their conversation, and how Caroline and Bruce began picking her brain about her latest Lily George novel.

But then the conversation took a turn that made Lou less joyful.

"You know, Lou's become somewhat of a Lily George herself around town," Bruce said proudly. "She's helped solve a few local murders."

Olivia regarded Lou, who was trying to gesture to her father to stop talking. When Olivia's gaze landed on her, Lou said, "It was nothing, really. I'm no Lily George, Dad. She's a detective. I just notice stuff other people don't, so sometimes I've been able to help."

Heat edged along Lou's cheeks. She'd divulged none of that to Olivia in their correspondence since she'd left the publishing company. It wasn't as if she was embarrassed, but Olivia was a former New York City cop. She was made of harder stuff. Easton and the Button police officers might humor Lou and accept her help here and there, but Lou knew well enough that it wasn't something larger police departments would or should do. Heck, not even all the Button officers were happy to have her help.

"Lou has an uncanny ability to notice things others don't," Olivia said. "You didn't tell me there had been cases you'd been involved with around here."

"There's one going on right now, in fact," Bruce said, making his daughter inwardly groan. "I keep trying to tell her we should help. The more brains working on something, the better. Right? And Lou's the one who found the second body."

"Second body?" Olivia's tone was flat with surprise. She pulled in a stiff breath, sitting rigid on the cozy couch.

Easton might laugh off her father's dreams of getting involved in a local murder investigation, but embarrassment crept over Lou as she thought about Olivia hearing his plans.

Given that he'd already said the worst of it, Lou tried to look on the bright side. At least Olivia was about to put her father in his place and tell him how bad it was when civilians tried to meddle in police affairs. As if Caroline could tell what was coming, too, she sat back and didn't cover up her grimace very well.

"Tell me everything." Olivia crossed one leg over the other. "What happened? I think it would be so thrilling to get involved in a case again. It's not something I missed, for a very long time after I left the force, but I don't know. This feels different."

"Well, the first body showed up all tangled in Christmas lights at the town tree lighting. And Lou stumbled upon the second one yesterday. Someone strangled him with an extension cord." Bruce's eyes went wide as he explained the events of the past few days.

Olivia's nostrils flared. "Are they connected?"

"That's what we need to find out." Bruce sat back, lacing his fingers behind his head.

Lou resisted the urge to close her eyes. This wasn't going to be good.

CHAPTER 8

"Don't you think we should get ready for the book signing on Wednesday?" Lou asked futilely as she followed her father and Olivia into Button Memorial Park after they'd closed the bookshop that evening.

After discussing the case in great detail, Olivia had decided they needed to check out the crime scenes to see if there were any clues left behind.

"The book signing will be fine," Olivia said, waving a hand to dismiss Lou's concern.

To be fair, Lou's worries weren't unfounded. Olivia wasn't a flake, necessarily, but public appearances weren't always her favorite and she'd bailed on a few book signings over the years. Those instances had mostly been when she was starting out and got nervous in front of the crowds but it had happened again a couple of years ago, so it wasn't completely out of her system. Because the woman forgot her phone at home more times than not, she wasn't always easy to track down either.

The last thing Lou wanted was for Olivia to get distracted.

"Yes, why don't we go back to the bookshop? We can help

you organize the orders, Olivia." Caroline jumped to Lou's aid. "Lou said she has quite a few preorders. Maybe you should sign some stock ahead of time?"

"There'll be plenty of time for that," Olivia said. "Right now, we need to focus on justice."

So that's what Lou, Caroline, Bruce, and Olivia were doing, tromping through the park, searching for clues along the tree line.

Olivia kept her eyes on the ground. "Stay sharp, Bruce," she said. "Anything around here could be a clue."

"Aha!" Bruce pointed to his right and scurried over to examine something in the grass.

Lou had to admit that the thrill of the investigation was getting to her a little. Her heartbeat ratcheted up as she chased after her father, stopping to peer down at what he was inspecting in the grassy field.

It was a lighter. Not one of those cheap, plastic ones either. The case was almost square, and it had a brushed finish on the copper-colored metal.

"Maybe the killer is a smoker." Bruce used a pair of kitchen tongs Lou was sure had come from her kitchen, to pick up the lighter and toss it into a reusable cloth grocery bag Olivia pulled from her purse.

Olivia tapped her finger against her lips. "We should make a list of everyone in town who smoked or would be likely to carry a lighter around with them."

Bruce handed Olivia the tongs and bag so he could jot down the information on a notepad from Lou's apartment.

After a few more steps, they stopped again. This time, it seemed much less likely that the item had anything to do with the case and that these things littering the field were just that: litter.

"This is a broken child's toy," Lou said flatly as she studied the neon fidget spinner that was missing one of its three spinning spokes.

"A child is usually *not* the murderer," Olivia conceded.

"Usually?" Lou laughed through the question.

"Put it in the bag anyway," Olivia said. When Bruce gawked at her like she might be crazy, she added, "It's trash, and we shouldn't leave that in the park."

"Hey," Caroline called from a few yards away. "This might actually be something over here."

The two sleuths and the reluctant participant, Lou, moved to see what Caroline had found.

"I can't tell what it is." Caroline tilted her head to one side and then the other, as if a different perspective might help her discern what she was observing.

"I think that's a money clip," Bruce said, kicking at the object with his toe.

Olivia picked it up with the tongs and studied it. "Yes, a money clip. This insignia must mean something." She turned it away from her so the rest of them could see the etched picture of a train in the middle of a circle with the letters BLS carved in an arc around the top half of the circle. "Bruce, write us a note to look this up later tonight."

"Should we really be taking any of this stuff?" Lou wondered aloud. "Don't you think we should leave it here for the police?"

She glanced around and noticed that there wasn't any police tape marking off the field as there had been yesterday when she'd come to meet Ferris. In fact, the maintenance building back by the parking lot was free of police tape as well.

Olivia scoffed. "Oh, sweetie. It's been—what—two days since the first murder? The police would've taken everything they needed from this area the following day, or it would still be marked off."

"Shouldn't that tell us that none of this stuff is important?" Lou asked.

"Or that it's even more important because the police overlooked it," Olivia countered. "Happened all the time when I was on the force." She squinted one eye. "Or maybe that's in my books." She shrugged. "Hard to keep them straight anymore."

In that way, they traversed the entire field and the area around the maintenance shed where Lou had found Ferris's body, trading off who used the tongs to pick up the different items. They had a full bag of items that mostly looked like trash, to Lou, including a Christmas ornament that appeared to have been made by a child, a deck of cards that was only slightly soggy from the dewy grass, a deflated ball, and three different fidget spinners, in addition to the broken one they'd found first. There were also many items that were obviously trash. The plastic lid to what looked like a peanut butter jar, a broken shoelace, a ripped piece of rose-gold leather, and a Christmas-light headband that had snapped in half.

As they turned back toward the parking lot, Lou remembered the magnet she'd found stuck to the fence. It was still there, in the same place she'd left it. Motioning for the tongs, Lou grabbed it off the fence, shrugging and plopping it into the bag her dad held.

"If we're already picking up trash," she said when her dad shot her a questioning glance.

His eyes sparkled with a suppressed grin. At least he was good natured about his daughter's reluctance to participate.

"When does the Christmas market start, honey?" Lou's mom asked, checking her watch.

Lou had almost forgotten. "Oh, we're supposed to meet

Willow at the bookshop in thirty minutes." Turning to Olivia, Lou said, "You're welcome to join us. This is my first time going, but everyone in town says it's full of great handmade gifts and art."

Olivia stretched her shoulders back. "Thank you for the invite, but I'm pretty tired from traveling today, and I should drop my stuff off at the inn, anyway." Olivia looked off in the distance.

"Are you sure you don't want to stay with Lou?" Caroline asked. "We have our RV and can move out of the guest bedroom for a few days while you're in town."

Olivia shook her head. "My publisher pays for the rooms, so it's really no big deal. Plus, the inn was very cute when I drove by it earlier. Some might say it's as cute as a button." She grinned at them.

Saying goodbye and splitting up into different cars, Lou and her parents drove back to the bookshop just in time to meet Willow for their rendezvous for the Christmas market that evening. It was way too cold to hold the market outside, so it was being held at the high school gym. The entrance was adorned with construction-paper winter scenes. Students, dressed like elves, greeted townspeople as they arrived. Christmas music blared through the school's intercom system, creating a festive feel.

"Ms. Grey! Ms. Grey!" A group of high school students—some elves, others not—raced over to greet Willow.

She hugged her former students, and Bruce went to pay their three-dollar entry fees.

"How's Willow doing with her decision to leave teaching?" Caroline whispered to Lou as they waited by the entrance.

"Good." Lou nodded resolutely. "I mean, it was a hard decision for her. She loved teaching."

"But this is what she needs to be doing for her soul," Caroline said in the same unwavering manner, knowing that to be true as much as anyone who knew Willow. "I hear the girls were pretty instrumental in helping her see that."

Lou's nieces had visited that summer and had done a lot of good, actually. They'd convinced Willow that she wasn't following her heart in a couple of aspects of her life, both by continuing to put her dream of owning her own nursery on hold and not admitting the feelings she had for Easton.

"Of course, when they told the story of their time here this summer, they were the only ones who could've gotten her to see what was right in front of her." Caroline rolled her eyes affectionately.

Lou was simultaneously overwhelmed with the feeling of missing her teenage nieces and loving that her parents were still in touch with the girls. They'd actually stopped by Montana a few days prior, on their way up to Washington. The Welsh and Henry families had done many joint-holiday get-togethers over the years, and they'd become just as close as any family. And even though Maddy and Mia had loving grandparents already, Caroline and Bruce were a welcome addition into their lives.

"She's looking forward to starting classes at the nursery once it opens," Lou explained to Caroline as Willow finally peeled herself away from the teenagers. "I know some of her students are missing her wealth of knowledge. The new teacher they got to teach horticulture this year is good, but if I had the choice, I'd want Willow to be my teacher too."

Bruce walked over, holding out a ticket to each of them just as Willow arrived.

"Shall we?" he asked, excitement ringing in his tone. He

loved markets of any kind—farmers, Saturday, craft, art, et cetera—but especially enjoyed a good Christmas market.

Lou's father was a man of many collections, and he was not only on the lookout for additions to the ones he already had going, but he wasn't opposed to starting whole new obsessions, especially now that he was retired and had the time. The only problem now seemed to be his lack of space in the RV.

As if reading Lou's mind, Bruce turned to her and said, "Did your mother tell you I've recently gotten into miniatures?" His eyes shone with delight as they entered the market.

Lou bit back a laugh. "That would make sense, given your space restraints."

The high school gym was packed with vendors, and they started on the left side, determined to visit them all. The large space smelled like a cinnamon stick, and they immediately discovered why as they approached one of the first booths by the door. The woman had created handmade bars of soap that were infused with all sorts of yummy Christmas scents. She had a cinnamon-and-clove fragrance, a spicy spruce tree scent, a frosted-cranberry variety, and even frankincense and myrrh. Between the group of them, they bought six bars, each excited about their own scent.

"No Olivia?" Willow asked as they put away their purchases and walked toward a handmade-pottery booth.

Bruce and Caroline walked ahead, admiring a grouping of wind chimes.

"She was a little jet-lagged from her flight this morning and wanted to head to bed early," Lou explained.

Willow eyed her suspiciously. "Wait. Why do you sound sort of relieved about that? Did things not go well earlier?"

Lou pressed her lips together, unsure of how to answer that.

"Lou." Willow dragged out her friend's name as if it were the truth, and she was pulling it out of her.

Lou peered over at her parents, who were busy with the wind chimes next door. "It's great to see her, but she got Dad all hyped about looking into the murder investigations."

Willow nodded in understanding. It wasn't as if she hadn't gotten herself involved in past cases, right alongside Lou, but now that she and Easton were involved—no matter how much she wondered how to define their relationship—it was harder to justify getting involved unless he specifically asked for their help.

"She even dragged us through the park earlier, searching for clues." Lou pinched the bridge of her nose.

Willow chuckled. "Did you find anything?"

"We have a bag full of garbage. Well, maybe not garbage, but it just seems like the town's lost and found. And if Easton didn't think it was important, I'm not sure why we should."

"That's interesting. I would've expected—"

"That Olivia would've known better, being a former cop and all?" Lou interrupted Willow with her guess.

"Yeah." Willow winced.

Lou wrung her hands to warm them up, even indoors, the winter weather was getting to her. "She's been off the force for almost twenty years now. Maybe she's forgotten what it was like. Though one would think she gets enough mystery and intrigue from writing her books."

Willow walked over to a booth that had crocheted headbands, coffeepot cozies, and scarves, in abundance. "Maybe she's bored with her writing."

"Maybe." Lou huffed.

Suddenly, a hand clamped down on Lou's arm. She jumped, only to recognize her father standing beside her. His eyes were wide with excitement as he swallowed, and she waited for him to speak.

"Don't all look at once, but the man over there with the metal yard art ... look at the flag hanging behind him in his booth." Bruce faced away from the booth and kept his voice low, like he was some kind of spy.

But immediately, Lou saw why. The market vendors used a myriad of items to block off their booths from the ones next to or behind them. The man with the metal art booth had used a large, green flag to act as his back "wall." In the middle of the flag was a drawing of a train with the letters BLS in a half-moon design hanging over the top, the same seal they saw on the money clip in the park.

"I'm going to go ask him what that flag is for," Bruce whispered before rushing over to the booth.

"Who is that?" Lou asked Willow once her dad was out of earshot.

She regarded the man, none the wiser as to the reason why he might be of interest. "Tom Rockwell."

"That's the man everyone was saying hated Arthur and talked to him before he died?" Lou asked, trying to keep herself calm.

"That's him," Willow confirmed.

Lou let out a thin laugh.

"What?" Willow turned to face Lou.

"This isn't going to help convince Dad to stay out of this investigation," Lou said, reluctantly adding, "I think our adventure in the park may have been fruitful, after all. Not everything we picked up was junk."

CHAPTER 9

Before Lou could say anything more, Caroline rushed over to Willow, pulling her toward a booth with gorgeous bouquets of fresh flowers, all made with Christmas-color schemes and adorned with sparkling red, white, and green ribbons.

Sure her father shouldn't be left to his own devices, Lou followed Bruce where he'd wandered into Tom's booth. Her father was doing a cartoonish job of acting "natural." He actually whistled as he pretended to peruse the pieces of metal art on display. Lou inwardly rolled her eyes as Bruce stopped and studied the flag until Tom glanced up in question.

"What does this stand for?" Bruce asked as Lou came over to stand next to him.

"Button Live Steamers." Tom stuck out his chest with pride. "We're a local group of railroad enthusiasts. We have a seven-and-a-half-foot-scale railroad that runs through Button Memorial Park. Our trains might be smaller than real ones, but they're powered by steam engines that are just as good as the big ones. We also provide rides for kids every Saturday."

Something clicked in Lou's mind. "Oh, you're the group putting on the holiday train rides on the seventeenth." She remembered that being on the town's holiday-event calendar and was also on their family list back in her apartment.

"That's us," Tom said with a dip of his chin. "It's our most popular event of the year. We have lights strung throughout the trees, and if it's snowing, it feels like you're in another world."

Lou studied the man. She wasn't sure if it was the passionate way he spoke of one of his hobbies, the fact that he created sculptures of birds, bugs, and cats out of recycled metal in his free time, or the knowledge that he was a widower that endeared him to Lou the most. But the man really didn't seem like a cold-hearted killer, someone capable of electrocuting an old business partner or strangling someone with an electrical cord.

Still, she saw this as an opportunity to get her dad to drop the idea that he needed to get involved in this case. And to do that, she needed to dig a little further.

"How many of you are in the Button Live Steamers Club?" Lou asked, feigning innocence when her dad gaped at her, probably surprised that she was asking investigative questions.

"Seven," Tom answered. "We're also the founding members." He let out a hearty chuckle. "Still haven't convinced any of the younger locals to get involved. I guess playing with trains is an old man's pastime."

As if he could tell what his daughter was trying to do, Bruce asked a follow-up question. "Ah, so it's a pretty select club?"

"Some would say that seven people is a lot," Lou said through lightly clenched teeth, hoping her dad would catch on that this wasn't good for his Tom-did-it assumption.

"And how many of those seven are men?" Bruce placed a

hand on the table Tom sat behind, leaning in close like a detective questioning a suspect.

He's trying to narrow down the number of club members who might've lost that money clip, Lou realized. It wasn't necessarily a bad tactic, since women didn't usually use money clips.

Tom barked out a laugh, then put up a hand. "I'm sorry. It's just, we've tried to recruit women. They just aren't interested. A lot like the young people." He'd obviously assumed Bruce's question was more about gender equality than an investigation into two murders. "No, all seven of us are men."

Seeing that her dad was still not dissuaded, Lou tried to ask questions that pointed out that the train-club guys would've had reason to be in the park other than to kill Arthur Crawford or Ferris Howe.

"I've only been to the park a few times, but I didn't see any trains there. Where are they located?" She ran her fingers across the rough edge of one of his metal birds.

Tom's eyes lit up as he said, "Tucked into the forest. If you walk past the maintenance building, our station is set up just past the tree line. But the tracks run all throughout the woods that border the park."

Lou's eyebrows rose. "You light all of that with Christmas lights?"

"Sure do," Tom said. "I usually also help with the town's tree lighting display." He winced, his mood turning somber. "Normally, we just do it all at once."

"Which meant you probably had to coordinate with the guy who took over the lights this year. What was his name?" Lou snapped her fingers as if it wouldn't quite come to her.

"Arthur," Tom said sadly. "Yes, unfortunately, I was setting up my lights at the same time he was."

Bruce shoved his hands in his pockets. "Were you there

when he…" Bruce didn't finish the sentence, but he didn't need to.

"I think I might've been one of the last ones to talk to him, actually." Tom scratched at the back of his neck in obvious discomfort. "My son had a meeting that went late at his office, and needed me to meet a plumber at his house, so I left around three." Tom clicked his tongue. "It's so awful."

Another customer slipped in beside Lou, wanting to inspect a metal woodpecker that one could attach to a tree. Lou moved, backing up until she was clear of the booth.

Bruce inclined his head toward Tom. "It was nice talking to you. Hopefully, we'll see you on the holiday train rides."

Father and daughter wandered away from the booth for a few yards before speaking.

"It sounds like it probably wasn't him, then," Bruce admitted with a hunch of his shoulders.

Lou hid her happiness at her dad's realization that they were grasping at straws. "Probably not. Plus, Easton's good at his job. He's got this covered. I promise, Dad."

Bruce wrapped an arm around Lou's shoulders. "Good, because I think this market needs one hundred percent of my focus. I'll have to let the case go." He squeezed Lou's shoulders against him as they turned down the aisle and walked in the direction Willow and Caroline had gone.

To Lou's absolute relief, her father really seemed to mean it when he said he'd drop the case. The next few days were full of writing Christmas cards and decorating the two Christmas trees they'd cut at a local farm—a small one for the bookshop and a tree for upstairs. Bruce and Caroline also attended their first play practice, which sounded like it would take up a lot of their energy.

Even more of a surprise was that Olivia, who joined them for most of the activities, didn't bring up the case either. Lou wondered if her dad said something to Olivia or if the woman was staying out of things on her own.

Either way, Lou was happy to have the full attention of her parents and friends on making fun holiday memories.

The whole family helped Olivia get ready for her signing. There were book orders to organize, which Caroline happily oversaw. There was a large display to create where the signing would happen downstairs, which Bruce put his crafting skills to work creating. And there were books to pre-sign in order to make the event go more smoothly, which Olivia really had to be the one to do.

By the time Wednesday evening rolled around, Lou felt like she couldn't have asked for a better few days. Not only had they gotten the first dusting of snow that morning, but the holiday spirit was alive and well in Button. It was the lovely feeling that had people smiling as they walked from shop to shop in the downtown area, bags full of gifts swinging on their arms. It was the warmth Lou felt when she heard a familiar Christmas song on the radio, or heard customers singing along as they shopped. It was cats curled up in front of the fire, or watching snowflakes drift down from the sky.

Lou was admiring the small Christmas tree they'd put in the corner, decorated in book-themed ornaments Lou and Ben had collected over the years, when Olivia showed up for the book signing; she wore black leggings, tall black boots, and a maroon sweater. The pop of color was something that didn't get past Lou. She knew Olivia was trying to branch out and wear something that wasn't monochromatic which meant she was taking this seriously.

"You look lovely," Lou said, pulling Olivia into a hug.

She smelled like cinnamon and cloves. Lou pulled back.

"You didn't happen to get new soap, did you?" She narrowed her eyes at the woman.

Olivia lifted her chin. "Your mother gave it to me. Doesn't it smell divine?"

Lou pressed her lips together. "I wonder where she got that?" she asked rhetorically.

"Now I'm even more upset that I didn't go," Olivia said. "She was telling me all about the clue you four discovered at the Christmas market."

Mom too? Lou thought with frustration. She needed to nip this in the bud. "If, by the clue, she meant evidence that Tom was not there during Arthur's death, and that money clip could belong to any of the seven members of the steamers club, then yes."

Olivia widened her eyes. "Right. And without Tom in the running as a suspect, tonight is even more important. We have to find some new leads."

"Tonight?" Lou gritted her teeth for a moment before adding, "Tonight is about your book signing."

Olivia waved a hand like Lou's words were annoying mosquitos buzzing around her. "I've done enough signings at this point that I could do this in my sleep. Don't worry. I'm good at multitasking." She kissed Lou on the cheek and walked over to the display table with her books, where Lou had set her up to sign and talk to the customers.

By the time they set up a station with coffee, tea, and a few small cookies from the bakery across the street, there was already a line built up outside. Lou had to put on her customer service smile, pushing away her frustration about Olivia and her parents' involvement in the murder investigation.

As the signing began, Lou focused on ringing up customer purchases while Caroline moved them through the signing line. Bruce was on cat duty, talking up the kittens and adult cats up for adoption. They couldn't let an opportunity with so many customers inside the shop go to waste. There might be someone in the crowd who could become a new cat owner by the end of the evening.

Olivia seemed to forget about the case, which Lou appreciated. She loved seeing her chat with each customer as she signed the books. Easton showed up in the line, holding up a copy of the book as he gave Lou a nonverbal greeting. She joined a group of customers fawning over the kittens.

A few minutes later, Easton sidled up to Lou, the same hardback tucked under his arm.

"Hey," she said with a smile. "Where's Willow?"

"On her way," he answered. There was silence for a beat before he asked, "Is there any reason that Olivia might've asked the guy in front of me if he knew of anyone in town who hated Arthur?"

Lou closed her eyes. Things hadn't been forgotten as she'd hoped.

"Or when I last saw someone use a money clip?" Easton added. His tone was hard enough that Lou knew he was frustrated, but it was soft, too, showing her he didn't blame her.

She opened her eyes and gave him a pleading stare. "I'm sorry. They're convinced they can solve this. It's like Nancy Drew in my house right now."

Easton scratched at his cheek, looking a little too pleased with himself. "I'm kind of loving that you're getting a taste of what I have to go through sometimes with you and Willow."

Lou groaned. "I totally deserve this, then, don't I?"

He chuckled. "Maybe not all of it. I'm dying to know what the money clip is all about, though."

"We found it in the park Saturday while we were searching for clues," Lou admitted with a grimace.

Easton cocked an eyebrow. "Did my guys miss something?"

Lou shook her head. "It was one item in a full bag of lost-and-found we came across as we walked through. I don't think it means anything, and I'm pretty sure your guys would've known as much, which is why they left it."

"They took pictures of the scene and anything of interest. I'll look through them again." Easton leaned away like he was already overwhelmed by the extra work. "There was a lot of garbage in that field, though. More than we expected."

"I expected more of Olivia," Lou admitted. "Being former law enforcement, I thought she would know better and leave you to do your job."

He raised his hands, palms up, seemingly unworried. "Willow said she's been a writer for almost as long as she was in law enforcement now, right?"

Lou confirmed that.

"She's probably forgotten what it was like. When she's the author, she knows how everything ends because she writes it. It probably makes her feel like she could solve anything. But it's different in the real world."

"So you're not worried?"

"Nope. But I'll take that money clip off you, if you want. If it's not part of the case, at least I can work on finding its owner." He winked at her.

Lou fetched the clip for him, putting it in a separate bag, careful not to get her fingerprints on it. While she was doing so, Noah walked up to the counter.

"What's going on over here?" He peered into the bag of lost-and-found.

Lou rolled her eyes. "I'm getting a dose of my own medicine." She explained to Noah what was happening with her investigation-happy friend and family members.

"And what does that have to do with fidget spinners and"—he squinted at the contents of the bag—"a student's Christmas ornament?"

"How do you know this is a student's ornament?" Lou asked, moving the bag so they could see the item better.

"Marigold made one of these too. I think their whole class did." He lifted the pine-cone ornament out of the bag. "At least everyone in Mrs. Little's class."

"Yeah, well, I think what we did was pick up garbage and lost items rather than find any clues." Lou couldn't help but chuckle.

Noah did, too. Once Noah placed the ornament back into the bag, Lou stashed it under the counter.

"I've got to bring this to Easton," Lou said, motioning to the smaller bag that held the money clip.

They parted ways, and Lou hoped handing over this potential clue would be her last time getting involved in the recent murders.

LATER THAT EVENING, Olivia approached Lou as she locked the front door. Caroline and Bruce were upstairs, preparing a late dinner for the four of them, but Lou and Olivia had a few loose ends to tie up after the signing.

"It's good to see you moving on, sweetie," Olivia said, wrapping an arm around Lou.

Lou blinked. "What do you mean?"

"That nice man, Noah." She said nothing more than that, but gave her a knowing look.

Ben had loved Olivia. He'd always appreciated her brashness, preferring people who spoke their mind. He didn't enjoy people he had to figure out, like puzzles. Lou had been frustrated this week with Olivia, but she agreed. It was nice when people told you exactly what they were thinking. Though, in this circumstance, it felt a little surprising.

"Oh, Noah and I are just friends." Lou felt her cheeks heat.

Olivia's laugh lines creased as she cocked an eyebrow. "Okay."

"Did you figure out anything for the case?" Lou asked, knowing she was desperate to change the subject, if she was encouraging Olivia to talk about an investigation she didn't want her to be working on.

Olivia's eyes lit up. "I did."

Lou did a double take, surprise making her cough.

"Tom wasn't the only one with a motive for murder," Olivia explained. "I heard Arthur got in a yelling match with someone else the morning of the lighting."

"Who?"

"That's the thing. The person I talked to didn't know. They just saw them get into a black truck and drive off. How many people in town have a black truck? It should be easy to narrow down..." Olivia kept talking, making plans about how they would figure out whose truck it was.

Lou tuned her friend out as she thought about the black truck that had peeled out of the parking lot the afternoon she'd gone to grab the pine boughs from Ferris. It had seemed suspicious at the time, and those worries were more pronounced now that it sounded like a black truck was connected to Arthur's death as well.

But she kept the encounter to herself. She wasn't going to feed the obsession with another possible clue. She also decided that she was done fighting Olivia and her parents about the case. If Easton wasn't worried about it, or threatened by it, she wouldn't waste her time on those emotions either.

Olivia stopped talking, possibly just to take a breath, and Lou took advantage of the break.

"If nothing else, you can use this as research for your next book," Lou said with a wink, hoping to make light of the situation.

Olivia agreed, and they headed upstairs to have dinner.

CHAPTER 10

The next day went by quickly in the bookshop. Lou's parents were helping with the play again that afternoon, so once Lou closed up the shop, she drove to Button Elementary. They wanted to hit the post office together directly after rehearsal was over.

Correction: Caroline wanted to go to the post office together. Lou still wasn't sure why they had to mail their Christmas cards as a family, but it was a tradition her mother had clung tight to over the years. Lou was sure some items on *her* holiday to-do list must seem silly to others, so she tried to humor her mother.

Lou parked in the school lot, but couldn't help but notice there was a black truck parked two cars down from hers. Was it the same one she'd seen peeling out of the park that day?

"Stop it, Lou. You're just as bad as they are." She scolded herself and then went inside.

The practice was just finishing up, and Lou stood along the side of the auditorium so she wouldn't be in the way of the parents leaving with their children.

The setting was beautiful. Painted backdrops of northwest pine trees and mountains worked as the setting for the play in addition to potted and hanging plants Lou knew were from Willow's house. The lush green ferns and potted trees helped give the stage dimension.

And it wasn't only signs of Willow that Lou recognized as she examined the stage. Many of the adults, and a few of the children, held color-coded schedules that outlined specifically timed events throughout the show. Caroline had obviously already been an immense help.

A song started on the other end of the gymnasium, including directions about how to put away their costumes correctly at the end of practice, and it had her father written all over it.

After standing there for a moment, Lou caught sight of Noah to her right. He was bent over, chatting with Marigold, who was still dressed in her Scrooge outfit—which involved a bald cap and an ornate robe.

She jogged off, calling a "Hey, Lou" over her shoulder as she left.

Lou stopped next to Noah, who watched his daughter with sparkling eyes. "Hey, Lou," he said, like his daughter, but without running away.

There was a moment of awkwardness in Lou as she thought of what Olivia had said last night. Noah was great, but Lou didn't know when she'd be ready to think about another partner again. Peggy Lee's words from a few months ago rang in her ears about her being young and not closing herself off to love.

She wasn't closed. It was just hard when she'd had such a lovely partner already, to think she could deserve something so good again. Equally difficult was knowing that not every relationship was as strong as hers and Ben's had been, and that she wouldn't be able to settle for anything less this second time around.

She stood next to Noah stiffly for that moment, not sure how to act. It was as if Olivia had shone a light on something that she hadn't known was there, and now it was all she could see. She didn't want to be awkward around Noah. He was a good friend, and part of her daily life here in Button.

"Here to catch a sneak peek before the big show?" he asked.

"You caught me." She snapped her fingers. "No, I'm meeting Mom and Dad. We're heading to the post office to mail our Christmas cards."

Noah scanned the crowd. "I saw them around here somewhere."

"I'm sure they'll turn up if I wait here long enough," Lou said to discourage him from trying too hard to locate them. They still had time before the post office closed. "How's the practice going?" she asked, hating that her voice still cracked with nerves.

Noah puffed out his cheeks. "It's going a lot better since your parents got involved. I tell you..."

He didn't finish his sentence, but from the stories Willow had told her about how chaotic it had been before, it sounded like the production could only go up from where it had been. She spotted a blonde woman chatting with one of the teachers off to the side of the stage, and Lou wondered if that was the talkative Julia that Willow was always complaining about.

"Caroline has us all on a tight schedule, one you wouldn't think second through fifth graders could keep up with, but then Bruce comes in with a little song including all the directions, and they're suddenly where they're supposed to be." Noah rubbed the back of his neck with his palm, like it was some kind of magic that equally scared him and had him in awe.

Lou grinned, feeling more at ease. "That sounds exactly like them. Dad always said that the best way to get anything done with five-year-olds was to put it in a song. Back in his classroom, he had a cleanup song, a wash-your-hands song, a good-morning song, and a goodbye song."

"Yeah, that man has a very specific skill for coming up with songs on the fly. He could take the act on the road. Just give him directions, and he can turn it into a catchy jingle that has the kids jumping into action as they sing along," Noah said. "I heard him singing earlier, and a line of children followed him like he was the Pied Piper or something."

Lou exhaled the rest of her awkward energy with a laugh. This was Noah. He was her friend, and one conversation with Olivia couldn't change that.

There were other parents milling about, and teachers were leaving, carrying bags full of papers and art projects to work on at home. Lou's mind returned to the black truck in the parking lot. On one hand, Lou knew she didn't need to get involved in the case, and had scolded her parents and Olivia for not being able to let it drop. But there was the same itching feeling to know the truth. Lou convinced herself that it couldn't hurt to ask. Plus, she still had yet to see either of her parents, so she had a few minutes to kill.

"That black truck parked in the lot out there..." Lou glanced over her shoulder, in the direction she'd come in. "You don't happen to know whose it is?"

Noah nodded immediately. That was the great part about living in a small town. Back in New York City, even in her apartment building, if she'd asked someone—that was, if she even dared to talk to anyone—whose bike or scooter was left in the hallway, they would've regarded her like she was crazy. But in Button, everyone knew everything about everybody.

"That's Robert Gavino's truck," Noah said. "Why? Looking to buy it out from under him? You converting to rural life and getting a truck?" he teased.

"No," she said with an air of fatigue, "but the Scooby gang I have hanging out at my apartment has been asking around about the murders, and they learned that there was a black truck seen at the park before Arthur died. They heard that whoever drove it got into a fight with Arthur, and therefore had a motive to kill him." Lou pressed her lips into a thin line before admitting the next part. "I also saw a similar truck leaving the park quickly right before I found Ferris, so it's not a completely unfounded wondering."

Noah's gaze flitted around the room a little more frantically than it had when they'd been chatting and observing the action going on around them.

"Noah?" Lou asked warily. "What does Robert Gavino do?"

He wrinkled his nose. "He's an electrician with A-Plus." He scratched at his neck.

"Oh gosh. I think that answers the question of where my parents are." She grabbed on to Noah's arm and pulled him with her. "We have to save the poor man."

"I'll check the classroom the kids are using as a backstage area. You look in the parking lot. We'll meet back at the main office." Noah split off to the right as Lou followed her pathway back out to the parking lot.

As if her worries had summoned them, Lou's parents stood in the parking lot, next to the same black pickup truck Lou had noticed on her way inside. A tall man with sandy-blond hair and a five-o'clock shadow stood outside the truck, his arms crossed defensively across his chest.

Lou messaged Noah, hoping he knew Robert and could help smooth over whatever damage her parents had already done.

"There you two are," Lou said, jogging over.

Her parents whipped around, surprise and a little guilt on their faces as they recognized their daughter.

"Lou, we were just coming to find you," Caroline said, sporting a smile too big for her to be up to any good. "And we ran into this lovely young man who was just telling us about his job with that poor guy who we saw hanging in those lights the other day."

Lou noticed movement in the truck's back seat. Two young children sat inside. Lou widened her eyes at her mom.

"Don't worry, they've got headphones on. They're watching a movie in there," Robert said.

And even though it did help that the children weren't hearing talk of bodies, Lou's worries weren't all the way assuaged.

"I'm sure this nice young man needs to take his children home after a long day." Lou said the last words through gritted teeth, embarrassed that her parents were so blatantly poking their noses into things.

Is this what I'm like when I investigate? she wondered with an inward groan. No wonder Easton, and Detective Anderson, for that matter, often seemed exasperated with her.

Robert said, "It's no bother. They were just asking me about whether I enjoyed working for Arthur. I don't mind talking about my job, especially now that my boss is gone." There wasn't a hint of sadness in his tone.

Bruce did a terrible job of hiding the wide-eyed look he shot

Caroline, and Lou coughed to tell him to cut it out before Robert noticed.

As much as Lou didn't want to jump to conclusions about the man, like she was frustrated with her parents for doing, the fact that he'd fought with Arthur before his death, and was an electrician, who would be in possession of the key needed to unlock the safeguard on the transformer, was all too much for Lou. Now that she was standing next to it, she was sure this was the truck she'd seen peeling out of the parking lot last Friday; it all felt too suspicious.

Lou gulped, really hoping the kids inside the cab couldn't hear through those headphones, because she was about to ask their dad if he'd murdered two people.

CHAPTER 11

Lou hugged her arms close, the cold seeping into her jacket.

Small piles of snow still sat along the sides of the parking lot of the elementary school, reminding Lou just how frigid it was. Robert had turned on his truck, so at least Lou knew his kids were warming up inside. And while the freezing parking lot wasn't her first choice for interrogating a suspect, she needed answers.

Before Lou could jump in with her line of questioning, her mother started in on her own.

"You didn't like Arthur?" Caroline asked sweetly.

At that question, a guffaw erupted out of Robert. "Arthur didn't like Arthur. He was awful to work with."

"In what way?" Lou chimed in.

Robert glanced up at the sky. "He micromanaged us, which was annoying, but the worst part was his inability to be flexible with scheduling. He acted like my kids were a burden." Robert's expression tightened with anger. "I'm a single parent—my wife split after Mikey was born—so if the kids need me, I have to be there for them. My parents help out a lot as it is, so I don't like to overuse them." He cleared his throat in discomfort. "Mikey has some difficulties, and I guess his mom didn't care to stick around for that. Anyway, he sees a lot of specialists, so either Luce has to come with us, or she gets dumped at my parents a lot."

Lou's heart melted a little. A single dad dealing with a kid with disabilities? But she had to admit that it sounded like he hated Arthur. It couldn't hurt to get his alibi for that evening.

Footsteps rang out behind Lou on the sanded parking lot.

"Rob. Hey." Noah came to a stop beside Lou.

"How's it going, Noah?" Robert raised a hand to greet the newcomer.

"Good. Good." Noah jerked his head toward the elementary school. "But we should probably let you and the kids go." Noah motioned to the truck where the kids were visible, watching their tablets.

Robert leaned against his truck. "They rarely get to watch TV because I save it for when I'm driving. Mikey's appointments are often in Seattle, so it's a bit of a drive. They're happy as clams in there." He chuckled. "Thankfully, we don't have anywhere to be today, so we get to head home."

"How often do you have to drive down to Seattle?" Caroline asked.

Robert kicked at the frozen pavement. "Every Wednesday and Thursday. Sometimes I feel like we should just stay there overnight. It used to be Mondays and Thursdays, so at least I felt like there was a break, but it's fine. He's getting the help he needs."

"Thursdays?" Bruce asked, interest lifting his eyebrows.

Robert nodded.

"So you missed the tree lighting?" Caroline asked.

"We left for Seattle right after school," Robert explained. "I didn't hear about what happened to Arthur until one of my coworkers texted around eight."

"But you came to talk to Arthur earlier?" Noah asked, proving he could let things drop about as well as Lou or her parents.

Robert bobbed his head once. "Just before I picked the kids up from school. I was trying to get him to give me Christmas off because of my kids. I thought I'd try one more time. If they were going to have to do Christmas alone with my parents, I was going to get them that kitten I've been promising them. Now, with Chandler in charge, I've got the day off." He shrugged like it made no difference to him.

"But then why were you at the park the next day, midafternoon?" Lou asked, jumping into the conversation and ignoring the questioning glares she was sure her parents and Noah were shooting in her direction.

Robert frowned. "At the—" His eyes opened wide. "Oh. That's a little funnier of a story." His cheeks turned red.

Lou wet her lips, and Noah leaned forward with interest.

"I was watching my niece that afternoon while my sister had a dentist appointment. I thought I could get away with buying her an ice cream cone downtown, you know, solidify my place as the favorite uncle." He smirked. "But Hailey didn't tell me she did an allergy test a few months ago, and they found out she's lactose intolerant." He scratched at the back of his neck. "We were on the swings when she told me she *really* had to go to the bathroom. I don't mess around with stuff like that, so I got her home as fast as I could."

There had been a few occasions when Lou's nieces had surprised Lou and Ben with an emergency restroom stop. Noah chuckled, probably having a similar story about Marigold when she was younger.

"How sweet of you to be a great dad and an involved uncle," Caroline said, her voice adopting a lilt that told Lou the lines of questioning were officially dropped.

"That's nothing," Bruce chimed in. "You oughta hear about when this one was four." He hooked a thumb toward his daughter. "Got sick in our brand new car and—"

"Dad," Lou said, cutting him off with the most stern tone she could muster without yelling. She adopted an uncomfortable grin, saying, "I'm sure Robert doesn't want to hear about that," through clenched teeth.

"And I'm losing feeling in my toes." Robert stomped his boots on the icy, snow-covered pavement. "It was nice to talk with you all." He held up a hand. "See you around, Noah," he said before turning to open his driver's side door.

"Rob," Lou said, stopping him as he was getting into the truck. "We have tons of kittens at the bookshop right now. Come with the kids, if you're free in the next few days. They're really sweet. *Even* if you have Christmas off."

He lifted his chin as he considered the information. "I might take you up on that."

The four of them waved to Robert as he got in his truck and backed out of the parking spot.

"Let's go inside. I'm freezing, and Bruce and I need to grab our stuff." Caroline rubbed her hands up and down her arms.

Lou followed. "So? Are you two satisfied he didn't do it?"

"Yes," Bruce said, but then he added, "though, I think we should check into this Chandler character. If he's inherited the company, a successful company at that, he might've wanted Arthur out of the way."

Caroline touched the tip of her nose. "Good thinking, honey."

"Chandler's been working for Arthur for years." Noah ran a hand through his hair. "Almost a decade, at this point. Everyone knows he's wanted to take over the company. But why now?"

Bruce fidgeted with the zipper on his jacket. "I don't know. Maybe something happened between them. They had a fight or something."

They opened the elementary school door and headed for the auditorium. Lou reveled in the heat, hoping she could defrost her fingers enough that she'd have the feeling back in them when it came time to drop off their Christmas cards.

Noah narrowed his eyes. "I'll ask around."

Lou cleared her throat.

"I'll, uh, make sure Easton's asking around, that is," Noah revised his statement, glancing over at Lou in apology.

She winked at him in thanks. "And we're going to hit the post office, so we can drop off the stack of Christmas cards we spent the last few days writing out and addressing." Her tone was just shy of forceful.

Lou's parents glanced down at their boots, like teenagers who were in trouble.

"I just have to grab my purse from the classroom," Caroline said, reaching in that direction, like Lou might not let her go if she didn't know exactly where she was going and what she was supposed to grab.

"I'll get our jackets," Bruce added, walking off in the same direction.

Once Lou and Noah were alone, Lou drew in a breath and

let it settle. "Is there a specific age when child and parent roles change? Because I'm really feeling like the parent around here." Lou finished the statement with a tired laugh.

Noah joined in, his dimples deepening. "Try working for yours sometime. I was helping at the quilt shop the other day and just *suggested* that they move on to getting a scanner and printer for their cutting counter tickets instead of handwriting everything, and you would've thought I'd told them to go clean their room." He shivered as if it was a scary memory.

Lou stretched out her fingers, finally thawing after her time outside.

"So I take it you haven't adopted out many of the kittens yet?" Noah asked. "I noticed you used the word *tons* when you were telling Rob."

Lou cringed. "Did I come off too desperate?"

"No, but if they're too much, I can find someplace else for them."

"It's not about them being too much," she said. "I just feel badly. I want them all to find homes for the holiday." She held out a hand. "As long as people are ready for the lifelong commitment and aren't just jumping into it because they want a cute kitten," she clarified.

"I know what you mean." Noah's lips pressed into a thin line. "What if we did an adoption event?"

Lou's eyebrows shot up as she listened.

"We could play on the fact that it's closing in on Christmas, and the kittens are named after the twelve-days song." He nodded as he spoke, apparently agreeing with his idea even more as he fleshed it out.

Lou agreed too. "That's a great plan. I could offer thirty percent off of their purchase of books if they adopt a kitten. That'll be great for people filling in the last few spots on their gift lists. What about this Saturday? The town's sure to be hopping with the gingerbread-house contest going on that evening. We could run the event from the time the bookshop opens until we close on Saturday."

"What about Saturday?" Bruce asked as he, Caroline, and Marigold approached. "Look who we found trying to write her lines on the inside of the sleeve of her robe." Bruce winked at Noah.

Noah knelt next to his daughter. "Are you still nervous you're going to forget your lines?"

Marigold's big brown eyes grew even wider. "Maybe," she said in a small voice.

Noah swallowed, then addressed Lou and her parents. "Some kid in her class was telling Marigold how glad he was that he didn't get the part of Scrooge because he would be embarrassed if he couldn't remember his lines, and how the whole school would see the mistakes." Noah's jaw clenched tight. "Now it's all she can think about."

Bruce knelt so he was closer to Marigold's height. "Ah, well, how about you come to the bookshop on Saturday? It sounds like there might be some kind of event happening. I can help you run your lines."

Marigold's previously worried expression shifted into a hopeful smile. "Really?" She glanced over at her father.

"We're going to have an adoption event at Lou's to see if we can't find some of those kittens homes before the holidays," Noah explained. "We'll be there most of the day. I think practicing your lines would be a great use of your time, on top of all the reading I'm sure you'll get done." He elbowed her playfully.

Marigold jumped up and down in delight. "Thank you, Mr. Bruce."

Together, the group left the elementary school, Noah and

Marigold heading to their home while Lou and her parents went to send off their well-wishes for the holiday season to friends and family. But Lou couldn't help but think about Arthur and Ferris's families. They were probably experiencing the darkest, coldest season of all, and no Christmas card could bring back their loved ones.

CHAPTER 12

The bookshop was abuzz that Saturday as Lou, her parents, the Romeros, and Olivia prepared for the adoption event. While things had gone back to normal when Lou had talked to Noah at the elementary school, being around him with Olivia watching once again made her rethink every gesture, all of her body language, toward him.

If she'd wanted a break, planning an adoption event with the man had been a bad idea.

Marigold brushed each kitten and made sure their collar colors were visible—the torties and black kittens had enough unique markings to tell them apart, but the three tabbies looked like triplets for all Lou could tell. Olivia had taken pictures of each one, and Caroline created little adoption profiles for each to hang in the window and around the shop, like Lou usually did with each of her longer-standing foster cats.

Bruce used his considerable craft skills to create a banner that they could hang outside, telling people there was an adoption event happening that day and advertising the deal of thirty percent off that went along with the kitten.

And by the time the shop opened that morning, they were ready to get the little ones off to good homes. Noah was on standby with the applications. It was Lou's job to sell books. Bruce had moved on to helping Marigold with her lines for the play. Caroline and Olivia had appointed themselves the adoption police, making sure people knew every cute thing about each of the kittens they'd gotten to know so well over the past week. Willow and Peggy Lee had wanted to attend, but they were finally meeting with someone who could fix the issue with the water leaks at the nursery site, so they had to prioritize that.

The place was hopping all day. Lou wasn't only surprised by the turnout but by *who* turned out. Not only were there families with children who came to browse, but many of Button's older residents came by to hold the kittens and see if any of them sparked a connection.

About halfway through the day, Lou noticed Silas, one of her regulars. She sidled up to him.

"Great event you've got here." Silas coughed as if giving her a compliment was uncomfortable for his grumpy soul. "I think I might be able to slip a kitten by the nurses in the front office."

His assisted-living home didn't allow pets, which was why Silas, who wasn't opposed to books but who preferred his daily newspaper, came to spend so much time at Lou's bookshop.

"I don't know if Catnip would allow that." Lou's gaze cut to where the white-and-orange cat was staring at Silas from under a chair in the back of the bookshop.

Catnip didn't like a lot of people as a rule, and the quiet pace of the bookshop was usually fine for her, but even Silas couldn't pull her out during a big event like this.

Silas smiled fondly at the cat.

An older gentleman came over to stand with Silas, passing him the second cup of coffee he held. Lou had seen him around town but had never learned his name.

"Lou, this is my old friend, Zeke." Silas wafted a hand from Lou toward the man who seemed to be dressed exactly like Silas, from his khaki trousers to the blue button-up underneath a Fair Isle knit sweater.

"Great to meet you, Zeke." Lou shook his hand. Although he wasn't a large man, his hand was akin to a catcher's mitt: formidable and leathery.

"I've heard so much about you," Zeke said, his light-blue eyes locking with Lou's. "I'm sorry it's taken me so long to make my way in here. But this seems like a great day to come."

Silas slapped a hand on his friend's back. "Unlike me, this guy is allowed to have a cat in his apartment, so I brought him here to peruse the selection." Silas's words dripped with sarcasm. And although Lou knew he was pretending to be jealous for the sake of a gentle ribbing with his friend, there was a hint of real envy below the surface.

Lou cocked an eyebrow. "Oh really? Where do you live?" She wondered if maybe Silas could move to the same apartment complex, so he could have a cat too.

"With my daughter and her family," Zeke said. "Just moved in this year, but they're gone all day between work and school. I've been thinking it would be nice to have a companion, and the little ones have been wanting a cat for years."

"Well, we're open until an hour before the gingerbread competition tonight." Lou gestured toward the pen of kittens. "So feel free to spend some time with them and see which one you have the best connection with."

Lou's interest caught on the kitten pen for a moment as she watched a teenager scoop up Drumstick and cuddle him to her.

Zeke took a sip of his coffee. "Gosh, it's going to be weird around town without Arthur, won't it?"

Silas rocked back on his heels. "It'll be different. That's for sure."

At the mention of the deceased man, Lou's focus snapped back to the conversation happening next to her.

"May he rest in peace," Zeke said, lifting his coffee in a cheers.

"He will, but everyone else around him in the afterlife will be the worse for wear." Silas lifted his own cup and laughed, coughing halfway through.

"You guys were friends with Arthur?" Lou asked, astonished.

They regarded each other and chuckled.

"No one was *friends* with Arthur," said Zeke.

"But yes, we ran in some of the same circles," Silas confirmed. "And I can say from experience that the man has always been as much of a grump as he was the day he died."

Zeke's eyes danced with memories. "Do you remember that first time we met?"

Silas's chin jutted back defensively. "Of course I do. How could I forget seeing you lose the love of your life like that?"

"Love of your life?" Lou blinked at the intense statement.

"Marla Jones," Zeke said dreamily.

"Marla Crawford," Silas corrected, dragging out her last name.

Lou's breath hitched in surprise. "You were in love with Arthur's wife?"

"Who wasn't?" Zeke asked dreamily. "She's still the most

fiercely smart and beautiful woman I've ever met." He scratched at his cheek. "Present company excluded."

Lou skipped over the compliment, more interested in his previous statement. "So you and Marla were a thing. What happened?"

"We were in love … until she met Arthur." Zeke shrugged.

Silas let out a guffaw. "She met Arthur's bank account, is more like it. She's still in love with you, if you ask me. But that woman loves money more than anything else in this world."

In all the talk Lou had heard about Arthur that week, none of which had been good, she had yet to hear much about Marla, his now-widowed wife. But considering everything she'd learned about Arthur's Scrooge-like tendencies and miserly heart, it didn't surprise Lou to hear that his wife was similarly addicted to the idea of money, or that she would make decisions on that basis alone.

Zeke nodded in concession. "She does enjoy the finer things in life. I was working in my dad's auto shop at the time and didn't have as many prospects as Arthur did. That was around Christmas when she and I met, wasn't it?" Zeke asked Silas.

Silas held up his index finger. "At the second annual gingerbread competition, I think."

Zeke huffed. "I thought she was the best Christmas present ever, especially for my parents, who'd been wanting me to settle down for a while." He mimed a knife stabbing through his heart. "And then she turned me down."

"You proposed to her?" Lou's eyes went wide.

Silas snorted. "After one day."

Zeke didn't seem remotely embarrassed to admit it. "She even told me why she was picking Arthur. Said she hoped there were no hard feelings, but she needed stability. Admitted she didn't even love him."

"I'm sure she grew to love him if they stayed married for this long," Lou said, glancing in between the two men.

Silas wrinkled his nose. Zeke stared at his feet.

"Well, now she has his money and doesn't have to put up with him," Lou muttered, keeping an eye on the checkout counter in case any customers wanted to purchase a book.

Zeke steepled his fingers together, holding them to his lips. "It almost didn't happen that way, though."

Lou cocked an eyebrow.

"It's a good thing we live in a small town." Silas clicked his tongue. "Word got around that Arthur would get almost everything they owned in a divorce."

"Not that it matters now," Zeke said. "She doesn't have to worry about any of that. She's set for life."

"And you don't think that's suspicious?" Lou asked, glad they were sequestered off in the corner, away from the adoption event.

Zeke scoffed. "Marla wouldn't hurt a fly. She's a queen."

Lou didn't share his opinion of the woman. "Had he always had that stipulation on their marriage, or was it a recent change?"

"New," Silas said. "Not sure how he did it, but it could be something similar to what he pulled with Tom."

"That was during Christmastime, too, wasn't it?" Zeke looked at Silas, who nodded.

"I thought Tom left the company willingly. He didn't cut him out." Frustration grew in Lou at the prospect of yet another inconsistency in the story she'd heard from the townspeople.

Both of the men grinned, then they burst out into another round of laughter.

"Tom left on his own. You're right." Silas bobbed his head. "Penny was sick, and he knew she didn't have much time.

Wanted to spend every second he could with her, so he told Arthur he needed out of the company, needed the money to help with their bills."

Lou tried to figure out where the whole "Arthur cheating him out of the business" came into play.

The men must've figured out they needed to elaborate because Zeke said, "It was what Arthur did after that. He did something with the books to make it look like the company's valuation was much lower than it was. Probably cheated Tom out of a hundred thousand dollars."

"But that wasn't even the worst of it," Silas said. "He and Tom had a whole understanding that Tom would be able to stay on with the company's health insurance for the rest of the year so that Penny could continue to receive the same health coverage she'd been getting up to that point."

"I'm guessing that didn't happen?" Lou asked, not sure she wanted to know the answer.

"Arthur took him off the plan and wouldn't discuss it with him." Silas looked down at his coffee as if the subject depressed him. "Tom never got it in writing, said he trusted Arthur, and it was just a verbal agreement, a handshake deal."

Zeke winced like that was the worst mistake someone could make.

"Penny didn't die because she didn't have healthcare at the end, did she?" Lou asked, realizing Tom might have a bigger motive than she first thought. Maybe she needed to check and make sure he really was with that plumber, like he said.

"No, no. Nothing like that," Zeke said.

Silas piped in. "Tom told me before that it just wasn't as comfortable for her at the end as it could've been, as he wanted it to be."

"Penny would never have complained, of course, but Tom

could tell she wasn't comfortable. Chandler too. They saw the end was rough on her. Tried their best to help her at home, but Tom always wished she could've been at the hospital with around-the-clock care."

"Poor Tom." Lou let the statement hang in the air, only glancing up as the front door opened.

Robert entered, Mikey and Lucy in tow. They scanned the shop until their gazes landed on the pen full of kittens. The kids raced over, doing a good job of slowing down so they didn't frighten the kittens.

Caroline greeted them and asked if they wanted to hold any of the kittens.

Lou smiled as the kids gravitated straight to Lord and Lady, two of the black kittens. She turned back toward Silas and Zeke. "Well, Zeke, you should probably get in there and pick your kitten before they're gone."

"I'll do that," he said, holding up his coffee cup toward her again and heading over to the kitten pen.

Lou walked around for a few minutes, stopping by Robert as he watched Mikey and Lucy cuddle Lady and Lord. "They're pretty set on those two, aren't they?"

Robert beamed at his children's broad smiles. "They knew right away. Thank you for telling us about this. They're going to be so happy."

Lou checked on her mother, making sure she wasn't within earshot. "Sorry about my parents the other day."

He laughed. "They're not the first people to make sure I had an alibi for Arthur's death."

Lou's lips parted in surprise. It had been so clear to her what her parents had been doing that day in the parking lot, but she'd hoped it hadn't been so obvious to him.

"Oh... I... That was..." She stopped trying to come up with

an excuse, simply studying him and saying, "I'm really sorry. They've got it in their minds that they're going to break the murder case wide open. You'll be happy to know that they cleared you from their suspect list."

"Don't worry about it," Robert said, good-naturedly. "I already went through it with Easton. I completely understand. And, as much as I hated the guy, I really didn't wish any ill will on him. Even if I did fantasize about him falling off a ladder more than once." He chuckled.

Lou wasn't sure that was a laughing matter.

"Hey," Robert said in a lower tone, peering from side to side. "If your parents are investigating who might've had a motive, Chandler has been wanting to take over for a long time. He also had a meeting with Arthur the day before the lighting about how Arthur wasn't stepping down, even though that had been their plan for the past year. Chandler was pretty frustrated with him."

Lou studied Robert's expression as if trying to discern whether he was telling the truth or why he would mention any of this.

As if he could tell what she was thinking, Robert said, "I didn't like Arthur, but that poor kid, Ferris, got dragged into this mess, and as much as I wanted to pop Arthur in the nose, no one deserves to be killed for their actions."

"But Tom said he had to meet a plumber at Chandler's house that afternoon because Chandler got caught up in a meeting that went late," Lou said. "He has an alibi."

Robert cocked an eyebrow. "Then why did I see him driving toward the park at the same time I was leaving town with the kids for Mikey's appointment?" Robert's kids called to him as they approached Noah for the adoption paperwork. "Just thought you should know," he said before waving and walking away.

Lou's mind reeled. Silas and Zeke's conversation about the way Arthur had hurt Tom and his wife might not mean much if Tom had an alibi, but Chandler might've had just as much cause, if not more, to want Arthur out of the picture.

It looked like Lou needed to confirm both of the Rockwell men's alibis. Because at least one of them seemed to be lying.

CHAPTER 13

Lou was more confused than ever.

She spent the rest of the adoption event in a mild haze, not able to let go of the clues she'd learned during her conversations.

Lou felt badly that she was in such a funk, especially since the adoption event turned out to be such a success. It had even begun snowing again, making everything feel even more magical.

Robert and his kids had adopted Lady and Lord. The teen Lou had seen holding Drumstick had decided to adopt him, a newly married couple had fallen in love with Partridge, and Zeke had created an instant bond with the quiet Milky.

Once they'd ushered out the last customers and locked the door, Olivia came over to help Lou take the collars off the remaining kittens. Noah and Marigold had gone home a few minutes before. Caroline and Bruce were upstairs, getting ready for the gingerbread contest.

"You look like you have a lot on your mind," Olivia said, running her shoulder into Lou's.

Lou sighed. "Am I that obvious?"

Olivia snorted. "After talking through book ideas with you for more than a decade, I feel like I can read your mind. I know your sighs, and I can tell when you're being silent because you're unhappy and when you're frustrated." Olivia examined her hands. "I know I've been pushing you beyond your comfort zone by getting involved in this case."

Lou couldn't hide her surprise at the turn the conversation had taken.

Olivia held up a hand, stopping Lou from saying anything kind or appeasing. "I told you, I can read you well. I knew you didn't want me or your parents to get involved. I'm sorry."

Lou accepted her friend's apology.

"Do you remember back when I quit the force, after you called me when I sold my first manuscript?" Olivia watched the kittens alongside Lou.

Lou hummed in response. "We met for martinis that neither of us could afford. Me, because I was a lowly admin assistant and you because you had two kids in college."

Olivia smiled at the shared memory. "I was so ready to be done with the force. I never told you this, but the day you called, I had just gotten back from a homicide scene." Olivia closed her eyes. "It was awful. Chills me to the bone to this day. I was so happy to be able to write full time and surround myself with fictional crimes instead of real ones."

Lou's heart hurt at the story. She knew how difficult it was for Easton sometimes, and Olivia had hinted at the emotional scars she'd picked up over the years on the force.

"But," Olivia said, wrapping her arms around her torso, "I think I started to miss police work a little this week. When I saw that friend of yours in action ... it's so easy when I'm writing a case. I can see the crime come together in my mind. I can follow the clues my character is going to find. I thought I could do that here." She swallowed. "But you were right. I shouldn't have gotten you or your parents involved."

Lou pressed her lips together, tight. She couldn't very well let Olivia apologize when she'd been spending the whole adoption event questioning people about the case.

"I'm the last person you should apologize to," Lou admitted before realizing she would need to elaborate. "It appears I can let the case go about as well as you and my parents can."

Motioning to the couch, Lou sat down for what felt like the first time the whole day. Olivia settled next to her, and within moments, Charles Lickens and Anne Mice had joined them.

"What did you learn?" Olivia's eyes sparkled with interest. "I mean, if you want to discuss it, to get it off your mind. But no pressure."

So Lou told her about how Arthur had not only cheated Tom out of money, but had made it so his dying wife wasn't afforded the same health care in her final days.

"Terrible," Olivia said, "but an excellent motive for murder. Though I can't figure why he would wait this long to get his revenge?"

"That's the thing. It doesn't seem like it was Tom. Although I haven't been able to verify his alibi, it's his son, Chandler, that has me more concerned. His son would have a pretty good motive to hate Arthur too. Tom said he was at Chandler's house meeting the plumber because Chandler got stuck in a meeting at work. But Robert says he saw Chandler driving toward the park at that time." Lou gave Olivia a pointed look. "And then there's Marla, Arthur's wife." Lou explained all about the information she learned about the impending divorce and the way she might've gotten around it.

"Considering the stories about her love for money, I

wouldn't put it past that one. I'd be happy to come with you if you want company when you go question her about her alibi," Olivia said, watching Lou out of the corner of her eye.

"Thank you for the offer," Lou said, meaning it. "But we won't be able to do anything about it tonight. We've got the gingerbread competition in less than an hour." Lou stood and picked up the carafe of coffee to judge how much was left. "Do you want to help me finish this? It can be like it was back when I lived twenty minutes from you in New York City."

"I'd love to." Olivia held out a cup as Lou split the last bits of coffee between the two of them.

Lou thought back to those early days in New York as she sipped. Though Lou and Olivia both eventually moved to nicer apartments after the success of Olivia's books and Lou's subsequent promotions in the publishing house, they lived just blocks from one another during the first few years of their working relationship. There had been a quirky coffee house about halfway between their apartments where they would meet to work—Lou reading manuscripts and Olivia typing away at her next novel. Lou missed those days when they'd been able to sit in each other's company while they worked.

Ben had always talked about how that was one way he knew they were good friends. He said friends are people you could talk to for hours and never hit a lull in a conversation. True friends, however, were people you could sit with, not needing to fill the space with words.

Lou's heart did a weird dance between love and grief as she thought of Ben.

Proving her earlier statement about how she could practically read Lou's mind, Olivia said, "You're thinking about him, aren't you?"

Lou smiled sadly. "How could you tell?"

"You always got that same twinkle in your eye when you would gaze adoringly at him," Olivia said.

Lou willed the tears she could feel building up not to fall. It wasn't as if she was afraid to cry in front of Olivia; it was just that she didn't always know if she could stop.

Olivia reached out, grabbing Lou's hand with hers. "I think I owe you one more apology," Olivia said when Lou looked up to meet her gaze.

"Olivia, you—"

She held up a hand, stopping Lou. "I know I don't have to, but humor me."

Lou decided to hear her out.

"I'm sorry for insinuating there was something going on between you and Noah. I'm not saying it wouldn't be fine for you to be moving on to someone else, but I understand everyone needs a different amount of time to deal with grief."

Lou inclined her head so Olivia would know that she accepted her apology. Her throat was so constricted with emotion, she wasn't sure words could get through.

"Ben was a very special person, and I know you're going to carry him with you for the rest of your life." Olivia patted her hand and pulled hers back. "I just need you to know that it's okay to find love again. It's not a betrayal of him."

Lou gulped. If anyone knew about that, it would be Olivia. She'd lost her first husband, the father of her children. Lou hadn't ever met Jasper, but he'd been a cop alongside Olivia and had been killed while on duty in a drive-by while he was on patrol one night. And as highly as Olivia talked about Jasper— not to mention his children remembering him as the very best man, just short of a saint—she'd met her current husband, Chuck, a few months after she sold her first manuscript, and it had been love at first sight.

Lou's heart ached at the thought of Ben, and for her friend, knowing the pain she was in when Lou had met her. It had been on the page of her first novel: Lily George, a detective, was on administrative leave after her partner had been killed when a drug bust had gone wrong. The raw emotion with which Olivia had written had been what had caught Lou's eye as she searched through the pile of manuscripts the publishing house received on what seemed like an unending conveyor belt.

"Rationally, I know that moving on is not a betrayal of him, but it sure doesn't feel like it sometimes." A hot tear fell down Lou's cheek despite all she'd been doing to keep them at bay. "I had such an amazing love story. How audacious of me to think I deserve another when some people go their whole lives finding nothing of the sort?"

Olivia nodded. "I think I said that same thing, sweetie. But it's not audacious. It's brave. Thinking of loving again is the bravest thing you can do. And it's what Ben would've wanted, for you to be happy."

He would've. Lou knew that. She was the problem. The issue lay within her. "But what if I'm not the right person for someone else, because I'm always comparing them to Ben?" Lou knew she could voice her worries to Olivia, given Jasper's saintlike existence and children who worshiped his memory. Chuck had big shoes to fill when they'd gotten together.

"You will," Olivia said. "Hopefully, you'll find someone who complements you in different ways. Ben brought out the extrovert in you. He pulled you off the couch and took you traveling instead of having your nose in a book all the time."

Lou held up a finger. "I mean, I still had my nose in a book. It was just with different scenery."

"You know what I mean," Olivia said. "You quieted him, and he lit a fire in you. That's Chuck with me. He makes me laugh.

We never have a serious moment. And he's what I needed, someone to help me see the joy in a life where I'd forgotten how to smile. You had that larger-than-life personality. Maybe what you need now is someone quiet." She fiddled with her coffee cup.

"Like Noah?" Lou asked with an eye roll, exasperated with her friend, but the action was mostly for show because Olivia wasn't wrong.

Noah was the opposite of Ben in so many ways. He was steady. It wasn't as if Ben hadn't been steady, but he'd been unpredictable in the best way, in the way that made Lou feel alive and always on her toes. But she was a different person now. She enjoyed the slower pace to small-town life and loved knowing what each day would bring—well, most of them, at least. To the person she'd become, steady sounded like the most perfect thing in the world.

Olivia shrugged, showing Lou she wouldn't push the issue anymore. "I'm going to go freshen up back at the inn and call Chuck. I'll see you at the gingerbread competition in a bit, sweetie."

"See you there," Lou said, watching her friend go.

She locked the door behind Olivia and headed upstairs to see if her parents were ready to go, her thoughts whirling around her like the snow dancing in the streetlights on Thread Lane.

CHAPTER 14

The annual Button gingerbread competition did not disappoint.

If Lou had thought the high school gymnasium smelled good during the Christmas market, that was nothing compared to the delightful smells coursing through the large space now. Scents like ginger, cinnamon, cloves, and allspice stung Lou's nostrils. But the sugary scents of molasses, icing, and cookie dough softened them.

The contest was made up of two different entry opportunities. The first was the "architect" level. These people had to submit their designs before Thanksgiving and had weeks to work on the project. They brought already created designs that would be judged against a rigorous list of criteria ranging from realism, architectural elements, size, and number of windows, to name a few. The winner would move on to the regional competition, which would be judged on Christmas Eve. If they won that, they would receive a prize package that was valued at over five thousand dollars.

The other option was the "artisan" level. Contestants at

that level would have two hours to construct their gingerbread structure. Everyone who competed would be given the same materials, and the person who was voted the best was crowned the king or queen of Christmas and would get to hand out the medals in tomorrow's Jingle Bell Run.

Caroline and Bruce hadn't been around in November to submit any sort of plans, nor did they have room in their RV to build an elaborate gingerbread structure, so they were automatically ineligible for the architect level of competition. Lou simply didn't have the time or patience for such an undertaking.

Her decision not to compete at that level was reaffirmed as she and her parents walked farther into the high school gymnasium. The "architect" pieces were beautiful, boasting intricately piped icing designs, melted sugar windowpanes, gingerbread toasted to just the right level of brown in the oven, and some even featured twinkle lights inside to give their display even more sparkle.

"Willow told me that there's a different theme each year for the regional competition," Lou explained to her parents as they wandered through, stopping to appreciate each individual design. "Last year was famous structures, but this year's theme is small towns."

Most of the competitors had opted to represent small-town life by displaying cottages or quaint churches. A few had attempted to emulate a specific building in Button, and Lou thought she saw a bookshop with cookie cats in the window.

They wandered through the architect section while they waited for Willow. She showed up just as they were peering inside a replica of the Bean and Button, the town's coffee shop that sat just across from Lou's bookshop.

"They even have little buttons decorating the walls, like in the actual building," Caroline pointed out, having visited the coffee shop more than a few times already during her visit.

"So cute," Willow said, leaning down to see for herself.

"Hey," Lou said. "How'd the watering stuff go today?"

Willow shrugged out of her winter jacket, looking tired but more at ease than she had all week. "I think we've finally got it figured out. I'm just glad I'm going through a winter with the nursery before I open so I can fix these little bugs that might really set me back once I'm open."

"Did Peggy Lee head home?" Lou asked.

Willow nodded. "She said she'd reached her limit of people today and couldn't see it going well if she was forced into a stuffy gymnasium with a bunch of cheery faces." She laughed. "How'd the adoption event go?"

"Great. Five kittens were adopted." She crossed her fingers. "Just seven more to go."

"That's great." Willow checked over her shoulder. "Hey, they were calling for the artisan group when I walked in a minute ago. We'd better go over there and get our supplies." Willow motioned to the other side of the gym.

"I'll be right there," Lou said, glancing down the line at the gingerbread house she swore was a miniature version of her bookshop. "There's just one more I want to look at."

Willow led Bruce and Caroline over to the tables where the quicker gingerbread houses would be created and displayed. Lou noticed Olivia joined them at the table. She hurried over to the gingerbread version of her bookshop. She'd been right. There were not only little cookie cat cutouts inside, but a few shelves with book spines added in icing.

"I hoped you'd recognize it."

Lou spun around to see George standing behind her, wearing an oversized black sweatshirt with the *Stranger Things* logo printed on the front. Her hair was pulled into two messy buns, one on each side of her head. Her outfit was finished with a pair of candy-cane leggings.

"You made this?" Lou blinked in surprise. "This is amazing."

The young woman beamed at the compliment. "I figured I spend enough time there, I should know it by heart now."

As George mentioned her time in the bookshop, Lou realized she hadn't seen her around as much the past weeks. Now she understood why. She'd been working on this masterpiece while Lou had been busy with juggling her parents' staying with her, an old friend visiting, and the possibility that someone in town had murdered two of their fellow citizens.

"It was the emporium or this." George gestured to the bookshop. "And your business is a lot cuter than mine."

George's Technology Emporium was a business the tech-savvy young woman ran out of her small home down the street. And as helpful as the whole town found it to have someone like George who could order, install, and explain how to use the technology, her method of keeping items in large plastic bins, stacked in her living room, was not exactly aesthetically pleasing.

"I didn't know you did"—Lou waved her hand at the gingerbread house—"this kind of thing."

"Every year since I was fifteen," George said. "I've always liked miniatures. I do a lot of really finite work when I paint D and D figurines, and I really enjoy it."

George's Dungeons and Dragons club met in the bookstore most Sundays, and Lou had grown to love listening in on the impassioned role playing.

"I think you're definitely in the running for the win." Lou surveyed the gingerbread bookshop yet again, noticing details she hadn't before.

But instead of getting a response from George, the woman standing next to the gingerbread structure to the right said, "Doubtful."

Lou drew in a surprised breath at the woman's rude comment, her wording even causing George to wince.

The woman, a grandmotherly-looking lady, wearing a red apron, covered her mouth with her hand. "Oh, I didn't mean it like *that*." She took a step closer. "It's only that now that Marla's allowed to compete, we're all doomed, no matter how lovely yours is, Georgie."

George nodded in understanding. "Thanks, Mrs. Milner."

Mrs. Milner and George focused their attention across the room at the section Lou had yet to peruse. Lou didn't have to search long before she spotted a tall woman, with gray hair that swooped into soft curls, standing next to a gingerbread masterpiece. She was decked out in a shimmery red dress and earrings that glittered so much, Lou felt like the twinkling might almost blind her from across the room.

Whereas most of the other architect-level competitors had opted for a very intricate and well-made single building, Marla had created a whole town block.

"Someone said she put edible glitter in her icing to get it to shine like that," Mrs. Milner whispered to George.

But Lou couldn't get past what the older woman had said prior to that. "Mrs. Milner, you said something about how Marla is *allowed* to compete. What did you mean by that?"

Mrs. Milner shot George a sidelong glance, telling Lou the answer to her question was neither pleasant nor short.

"Last call for gingerbread artisans," a man called from across the gym.

Lou chewed on her lip, considering the table where her

parents, Willow, and Olivia had settled. They had all their supplies ready and were chatting away as they waited.

"Sorry," Lou said, pulling out her phone. "Can you hold that thought for just one moment?" She made a group text with her mom, her dad, Willow, and Olivia, and sent a message.

> Got caught up talking with George. Not going to do the competition. I'll come over to see how you are doing in a few.

After hitting send, she watched as Caroline noticed her phone first—mostly because the volume on her ringer was practically maxed out at all times—then Bruce and Willow pulled out theirs. Olivia didn't move, and Lou realized with a chuckle that the woman had most likely forgotten her phone back at her room at the inn. The rest of the table read the message, conferring for a moment before turning to find Lou. She waved at them to show them she was okay, and after waving back, they turned to their supplies, ready to create.

"Okay, Mrs. Milner. Now I'm ready to listen." Lou gave her attention to the woman.

"Call me Heidi, dear." Heidi checked over her shoulder to make sure no one was behind her. "This is the first year Marla has competed in decades, ever since she married Arthur."

Lou remembered Silas and Zeke talking about the first Christmas they met her, at the gingerbread competition. "He wouldn't let her compete?"

George and Heidi shook their heads in tandem.

"Hated everything about Christmas, and didn't like her to get involved either," Heidi explained.

"Whoa," Lou said. After a moment, she asked, "Was there something in Arthur's past that caused him to be so against the season?"

She couldn't help but think of Dickens's character, Scrooge. And while the man was meaner than he had any cause to be, and learned that he needed to change his ways, there were past events that had led to his sour attitude. Now that she thought about it, Lou wondered if something from Arthur's past was what had gotten him killed.

But as she looked to George, then Heidi for the answer to her question, she was met with apologetic grimaces.

"I would love to say that there was some bigger reason behind the man's sourness," Heidi said. "But I think he's just the example of what happens to a person when they choose money over anything else, repeatedly." Heidi clicked her tongue in disappointment.

Mentally, Lou added *controlling* to the growing list of motives she'd started for why Marla might have wanted Arthur out of the picture. A husband was one thing. What about Ferris? His only crime was seeing too much—well, and possibly blackmail, if what Lou had overheard on Easton's call was true.

"And even if she was miserable, she couldn't divorce the man," George said, proving Zeke wasn't the only one who'd heard about Arthur's plans to leave Marla with as little as possible in the case of a divorce.

Lou thought about Zeke's infatuation with her. "It seems Arthur wasn't the only one who consistently chose money over people."

After all, that was what it all came down to: Marla had chosen Arthur, ironically because of the money he wanted to leave her without in his wake. She, like her husband, was the creator of her own prison. But, unlike Arthur, she'd been cornered.

Lou studied the impeccably dressed woman across the

room and wondered if she would kill two people just to get the freedom she so desperately wanted.

CHAPTER 15

Lou had only just waved goodbye to George and Heidi to go check on how her family was doing with the gingerbread competition, when she walked straight into Olivia, who'd been coming her way.

"You're done already?" Lou craned her neck around Olivia to check for herself as to the state of her gingerbread creation.

It was ... technically a house.

A shudder moved through Lou before she could stop it. "Oh, nice," she said diplomatically.

Olivia snorted. "I know it's terrible. But I saw you over here whispering with George and Mrs. Claus, and I felt like I was missing out on all the fun."

"Mrs. Claus?" Lou stifled a laugh. She had to admit that Heidi Milner *did* look a lot like the fictional character, considering her rosy cheeks and red apron. "I wouldn't call the conversation we had 'fun.' It was mostly George and Heidi giving me one more reason to believe Marla killed her husband." Lou jerked her head over toward where the recent widow stood next to her gingerbread display.

To Lou's surprise, Olivia grabbed on to her arm and started walking. "Okay then, let's see if we can't get her to spill the truth."

Mouth parted, Lou thought about protesting, but she recognized Olivia's look of determination. She was on a mission.

It couldn't hurt to talk to her, Lou rationalized as they approached the amazing gingerbread scene and its creator. *Plus, this is the perfect time because we can use the gingerbread house as an opening.*

So by the time they stopped in front of Marla and pretended to be interested in her gingerbread creation, Lou had a few questions stacked up in her mind. While she contemplated which would elicit the most information, Olivia took charge.

"This. Is. Amazing." Olivia marveled at the gingerbread masterpiece in front of her.

At least her comments didn't seem like an act. Olivia genuinely sounded impressed with the structure Marla had created.

"Thank you." Marla's cheeks reddened from the compliment.

"No, really. You should see the atrocity I just brought into this world." Olivia motioned toward the table where her gingerbread house sat. "This is on a whole different level."

Marla laughed.

Lou hadn't seen Marla laugh, or even smile, since she'd been watching her that evening. Lou stood back, content to let Olivia work her magic.

"You probably win every year, don't you?" Olivia straightened from where she'd been stooping to get a look inside the frosted candy windows.

At that comment, Marla's smile dropped. She caught it,

securing it back in place a moment later, but the slip hadn't escaped either Lou or Olivia's notice.

"Oh, this is actually my first time competing in ... years," Marla said, exhaling like she'd forgotten how much work it could be.

"Why's that?" Olivia asked. "Are you not from around here, like me?"

Marla pursed her lips. "No. I-it's complicated."

Olivia crossed her arms and waited, as if the phrase "It's complicated" was a universal precursor to someone opening up to tell an exciting story, instead of being synonymous with "I don't really want to talk about it."

Bold as her actions were, they worked.

Marla cleared her throat. "My husband didn't really enjoy the holidays. But he just passed last week."

The detail-oriented part of Lou's mind latched on to that sentence. "Wait. But didn't you have to submit your plans weeks ago?" Lou's pulse hammered in her ears, and she could feel Olivia stiffen next to her. That could be the proof they needed to show that Marla had committed premeditated murder.

Marla's flighty gaze snapped up to meet Lou's. Her innocent blue eyes turned stony. "The judging panel made an exception for me because of the circumstances." Marla's words came out tight.

"Wow. Then all the more kudos to you." Olivia cocked her head, impressed. "You did all of this in a fraction of the time everyone else had."

Marla pushed back her shoulders. "I did. Thank you. It was a nice distraction from everything else this week." Her eyes moved around the space, a sure sign that she was looking for a way out of the conversation.

They needed to steer the subject back to something pleasant, or they were going to lose her. Thankfully, Lou had used the time while Olivia was talking to study the gingerbread town Marla had created. And something tiny, probably insignificant to anyone else, had caught her eye.

"Is that a little kitten in the window there?" Lou peered inside, illuminated with twinkling fairy lights.

Marla's entire face lit up as if it had its own string of fairy lights. "That's my favorite part of the entire piece." She leaned forward to look at it as if she hadn't been the one who made it.

"It's so cute," Lou cooed. "Is this based on your cat?"

Lou wasn't really sure where she was going with the conversation. She was simply trying to buy them more time to talk, and she could talk cats … well, for as long as she had breath.

"No." Marla's tone dipped. "I don't have a cat." She wrinkled her nose. "The husband, again. He didn't like them."

Lou bristled at the comment. She knew not everyone was as big of a fan of the animals as she was, but when added to the long list of negative characteristics people used to describe Arthur, it only made her dislike him more.

"Well, you can get one now. Can't you?" Olivia said.

Marla's eyelids fluttered in a series of surprised blinks. If Lou had been drinking anything at the time, she would've choked on it because she sucked in a breath at her friend's blunt comment.

Olivia sent them both sidelong glances. "What? You couldn't do holiday things, but now you are. You couldn't have a cat, but now you can." Olivia smiled, not missing a beat. "And I know just the place for you to find the perfect one. This girl has a bookshop full of the cutest, nicest felines you'll ever meet.

You should swing by some day. Sweetie, give her your card." She snapped her fingers at Lou.

Lou stared blankly at her friend. "I don't have a card. I mean, I have bookmarks back at the shop, but"—Lou scratched at her temple—"it's called Whiskers and Words. It's on the corner of Thread and Thimble."

Olivia grunted out a laugh. "You're kidding, right?"

Lou shook her head.

"This town is too cute." Olivia turned her attention back to Marla. "Anyway, there you go. It's on the corner of sugar and spice, you heard her. Come by. There are kittens galore romping around the shop."

Marla nodded. It started out slowly, an edge of reluctance in the gesture, but then she built speed. "I will. Thanks," she said, waving at the two women.

Lou suspected that was enough of an *I'm done talking* sign as they were going to get, so she and Olivia pretended to move on to look at the other gingerbread house entries. But Lou couldn't help but deflate a little as they walked on.

"What?" Olivia asked her, whispering and checking over one shoulder.

"We didn't learn anything helpful." Lou's shoulder slumped forward in defeat.

Olivia held up a finger. "Ah, but we bought ourselves more time. That's the key. Now we know she's going to come to your turf, and you have time to think about what questions you definitely need to know for that adoption application of yours." Olivia smirked.

"First of all, turf?" Lou asked in amusement. "This isn't a rumble. And second, the application doesn't have questions like, What were you doing between the hours of three and five, Thursday, December first?" Lou rolled her eyes.

Olivia let out a dramatic exhale. "Yes, but you *could* ask things like, What's your weekly schedule? And say it's to make sure she's not a workaholic who's going to leave her poor kitten home alone all day. It's not exactly what we want to know, but it might help you rule her out if she says something like, I braid straw into gold every Thursday evening from four until nine." Olivia said that last part in an almost perfect Marla impression —maybe a little snottier sounding.

Lou considered the idea. "Actually, that could work." She continued walking, appreciating a particularly cute miniature of the town sweetshop, Candy Buttons. "You know, it's almost like you used to be a cop, or something." She elbowed her friend playfully.

"Or that I write about investigations all day," Olivia teased. "Okay, in the meantime, you need to think about the other suspects on your list. We should see if someone can verify this plumber story Tom gave you, but I'm more interested in this information about Chandler." Olivia twiddled her fingers.

"Me too." Lou lined up the clues she had gathered against him. "He could've been harboring anger toward Arthur this whole time about how he treated his father, and especially his mother. Robert, the electrician, also said Arthur was supposed to step down, leaving the company to Chandler, but he'd recently changed his mind." Lou took a long breath, having exhausted herself with the extensive list.

Olivia blinked. "Why did we just waste so much time talking to Marla, again?" she teased. "This Chandler guy seems like our top suspect. We need to find out if he can get someone to substantiate this claim that he had a meeting."

Lou nodded, and the two of them scanned the gym.

"I'm hoping you know what he looks like, because I don't have a clue," Olivia whispered a few seconds later.

Lou chuckled. "Don't worry. I know what he looks like, but I don't see him here. Tomorrow's the Jingle Bell Run, though. I've heard there's a huge turnout. We can check then."

Olivia narrowed her eyes. "It's a plan."

CHAPTER 16

The Jingle Bell Run was set to start at nine the following morning. By eight, Lou was dressed in her warmest running gear and had already started jogging around the bookshop and stretching to keep herself warm.

The older cats hid, shying away from her quick movements, but the kittens followed her with wide, mischievous eyes, like they would be chasing her around the shop if they weren't still in the pen.

During one of her hamstring stretches, Caroline approached Lou with a necklace made of jingle bells and a headband with reindeer antlers glued on to it. She slid the necklace over Lou's head and then settled the antlers on next.

"Are you sure you two don't want to come with me?" Lou asked, sending one last pleading glance in her father's direction.

Caroline shook her head. Bruce let out an "Oh, goodness no" that was mixed with laughter.

"We'll stay here and watch the shop for you, so you don't

have to close." Caroline tucked a strand of hair behind Lou's ear affectionately.

Willow had called that morning, complaining of a stomach bug, but she sounded very sure it would clear up that afternoon sometime.

The front door opened, and Olivia entered.

"At least Olivia will go with me." Lou beamed at her friend.

Olivia took a moment to shiver out of her thick winter jacket and made a show of shaking off the cold weather before moving inside. "Sorry, kid. Not a chance. It's freezing out there." She rubbed her hands up and down her sweater-clad arms.

Lou placed a hand on her hip. "Says the woman who's used to harsh New York winters. This isn't worse than that."

"Touché," Olivia said, adding, "I'm still not running with you. You've got this one on your own." Olivia winked, showing Lou she hadn't forgotten about the idea to question Chandler during the race like they'd discussed last night.

Grabbing her running jacket, Lou accepted her fate of being the lone runner from the shop that morning. "Okay, well, I'm going to head to the starting line." She shimmied into her jacket and gave her antlers an extra jingle before she slipped out the front door into the frosty morning.

She pretended to be exasperated by her family and friends' lack of participation, of course, but once she got outside, Lou felt exhilarated. She was going to find Chandler Rockwell and see if she could get the truth about the man's alibi for both the time Arthur had been killed, and that Ferris had been taken out for seeing too much. If he showed up for the run, that was.

Lou couldn't look past the overwhelming evidence that some people weren't so keen on running in winter—or in general. She was the only one running out of her family, after all.

Thinking back to when she'd seen Chandler at the infamous tree lighting, she thought he'd appeared to be in good shape, like a person who would want to take part in a jogging-based Christmas tradition. And Lou wasn't disappointed as she gathered in the large group of equally jingled-out runners near Button Lake. Chandler Rockwell stood at the front of the pack, stretching out his quads.

Oh, so he's a front-of-the-pack runner, Lou thought, metaphorically rubbing her hands together in anticipation of a challenge.

Noah, Cassidy, and Marigold wore matching elf costumes, and Lou waved to them, but she positioned herself in the front, so she wouldn't be tempted to talk to them and get distracted from her mission. She was confident that getting Chandler talking while he was running, even if he was as fit as he seemed, would still work in her favor. He was much more likely to give up information if he was distracted or slightly out of breath.

Also, at the front of the group with Lou and Chandler was Officer Brenner, Button PD's newest officer. Well, officers. Plural. Because along with Officer Brenner came his partner, a bloodhound and Labrador retriever mix named Peanut Butter. The town still wasn't sure what they would need a K9 unit for, but they were happy to have them. Officer Brenner wore a full Santa suit, while Peanut Butter was dressed up like Rudolph until he immediately pawed off the red nose.

"Runners ready?" Mayor Teller Edwards called through his same loudspeaker from the other night.

The crowd responded, the cheers mixed with one loud exclamation of, "Ho, ho, ho" from the middle of the group. With an enthusiastic jingle of the bells he held, the mayor started the race.

While the roads had been plowed and were shut down for

the forty-five minutes allotted for the run, Lou spent the first block getting into her stride and focusing on her breathing. It was still icy in places, and even though she'd warmed up and stretched, she wasn't about to get complacent and hurt herself. She'd spent the last twenty years running through the frozen pathways of Central Park, so she knew how quickly a foot could slip and leave behind a large bruise, or worse.

Safety taken care of, Lou scanned the group running around her, for Chandler. The route was just over three miles, a true five-kilometer run, so while she had a little time before the finish line, the sooner she got the conversation started, the better.

The only problem was, she couldn't see Chandler Rockwell anywhere.

Had he already passed her? There were a few high schoolers who Lou was pretty sure were on the school track team, who'd blown past in the first few minutes of the run, but she would've noticed if Chandler had overtaken her, right? As the group came to the first corner, Lou squinted and peered down Spool Avenue, searching for the bright yellow vest Chandler had been wearing.

She just caught sight of the small group of high schoolers as they took the next corner onto Needle Street, but there was no sign of Chandler.

Lou slowed her pace. She'd always been the slower runner between her and Benjamin, so she usually assumed most people were faster than her, especially when they acted with the confidence she'd seen in Chandler before the run.

Even as she slowed, she couldn't find Chandler. Feeling ridiculous, Lou moved to the side of the road, stopping to pretend to tie her shoelace so she could watch the runners pass by. As keenly as she was watching the runners, scanning for a hint of the bright yellow vest, a commotion behind her on the sidewalk pulled her attention away.

Lou had stopped right in front of the town garden supply shop, Glove and Trowel. A sign in the window boasted a Christmas Sale, and from the crowds of people milling about inside and looking through the items on a sidewalk sale, the discounts must've been fantastic.

She was about to turn back to the runners, to do another scan for Chandler's yellow vest, when something in the window caught her eye. Suddenly, she knew she'd found the solution to Willow's Christmas gift woes. But before she turned away, she noticed a sign on the item that said Last One in Stock!

If the place hadn't been positively buzzing, Lou might not have worried about it at all, but if that really was the last one, and someone snatched it up before Willow, Lou would never forgive herself.

Glancing once over her shoulder, she hopped onto the curb and slipped inside the shop. The store was large, about the same size as the expansive Material Girls quilt shop, housed in the building behind. Instead of holding bolts of fabric and the humming sound of sewing machines hard at work, the garden shop smelled faintly of fertilizer and held the pleasant sound of a trickling fountain somewhere in the back.

Lou snatched the large box, holding it awkwardly as she took it over to the register.

"I'm so sorry, but I'm part of the Jingle Bell Run"—Lou struggled with the box, holding it in one arm for a moment so she could point to her antlers with her free hand, as if the woman needed proof—"so I can't buy this at the moment, but is there any way I can put it on hold?"

The woman behind the counter looked like the large number of customers crowding the shop already overwhelmed her. After a beat, however, Lou's request seemed to register, and she said, "Oh, sure. Let me just get your name, and I'll hold it behind the counter for you."

Grateful, Lou set down the box and slid it toward the woman. "My name is Lou. I own the bookshop around the corner. Okay, I've gotta run."

And with that, she jogged back out into the street, rejoining the runners. Lou had been stopped for long enough that she was at the section of the crowd who opted to walk the distance instead of running.

She chewed on her lip. While Chandler hadn't been as fast as her, she doubted he was walking if he'd started at the front of the group. Which meant he must've passed by while she'd been inside the shop.

Getting back into her pace, Lou jogged through the group of walkers. She was probably annoying everyone, but she jogged in a sort of large zigzag, from one side of the road to the other, as she made her way through the walkers and into the slower joggers. She passed by Officers Brenner and Peanut Butter, but it looked like the K9 officer was more interested in sniffing everything than doing any jogging.

Still, there was no sign of Chandler or his bright yellow vest, even after Lou crossed the finish line a little while later. She was breathing heavily from the run, and the winter air stung at her lungs. The sigh of disappointment she wanted to let out after realizing she might've missed her chance to talk with him didn't even feel satisfying.

At least she'd found the gift for Willow. That was something positive.

And who knows if he would've even talked to you anyway, Lou told herself, trying to make the best of the disappointing situation.

Focusing on the good, Lou pulled out her phone and called Willow.

"Hello," Willow answered. The sound of a horse snuffling and stamping his hooves in the background told Lou that she was at the barn with OC.

"Drop everything you're doing," Lou ordered.

Willow faked a cough. "I'm sick. Remember? I can't do the run with you. I'm so sorry."

"I thought it was a stomach bug," Lou teased.

"Uh, right, yeah. I think maybe the cough is something on top of that," Willow scrambled.

"Willow, you don't have to fake being sick anymore. I'm done with the run. I want you to meet me at the Glove and Trowel. I've found the perfect gift for you to give to Easton."

"Really?" Willow asked. "What is it? No. Wait. Don't tell me. I want to be surprised. I'll be right there." And with that, Willow hung up the call.

LOU ONLY HAD to wait five minutes before Willow parked on the street outside and jogged into the shop. In that five minutes, Lou had accumulated quite a few items to buy. While the crowds had dissipated some since she'd finished the run, the place was still busy. Lou clutched her purchases to her chest as if one of the other customers might steal them away from her.

"Hey," Willow said, panting from hurrying over. Her gaze flicked over to the stack of items in Lou's arms. "I'm getting him all this?" she asked warily.

"No, but I found the last few gifts I needed to complete my shopping list. *I'm* getting these." Lou set down her items on the counter and waved a dismissive hand at the pile of stuff, showing Willow she didn't need to bother looking at it. "*This* is what I wanted you to see." She wafted her hands toward the box behind the counter she'd set aside for Willow—or rather, for Easton—as if it were a vowel on Wheel of Fortune.

Willow placed her hand on her hip and cocked her head as she took in the garden-bed-covering system. While it was merely a structure and netting, the piece symbolized so much more. Willow might be the person with the greenest thumb that Lou knew, but Easton wasn't a slouch in the garden either. In fact, he had a rather robust vegetable garden, one that Willow's horse often liked to sample when he inevitably escaped from his paddock.

OC, short for Of Course—because a horse is a horse, of course, of course—was as mischievous as he was gorgeous. Even though Willow turned him out into the grassy garden area between her house and the barn daily, the chestnut gelding often broke out of his paddock when she was out. Despite the low fencing between Willow and her neighbor, OC could reach his long neck across into Easton's garden.

It had been a continued matter of strife between them, until Easton had admitted that he didn't mind the horse's pilfering, especially when it meant he got to talk to Willow. OC was not the only creature who tried to beat Easton to his homegrown food, however, and Lou knew he'd been searching for a solution for years. He'd talked at length about building a netting system himself, but being a busy detective had occupied most of his time, and when he had time off, he liked to use it to fish or relax with Willow, now that they'd been seeing each other.

"Lou, you did it." Willow shook her head in awe.

Lou felt that same lightness spread throughout her chest.

"It's perfect," Willow continued. "It's cute because it high-lights the thing that brought us together, so it'll work as a more romantic gift if he gets me something along those lines. But it's also casual enough that I could just say I bought it for him in more of a neighborly capacity if he doesn't get me a gift."

Pride expanded through Lou like the warmth from a sip of hot tea. She knew the gift dilemma had been weighing on her best friend, and she was happy to help. They paid for their items and exited the shop. Willow clutched the large box as if it contained something dipped in gold.

"I cannot thank you enough." Willow peeled one arm off the box and wiggled her fingers, signaling for Lou to come nearer.

When Lou did, she smooshed her into a hug, the box clutched between them.

"Happy to help," Lou said.

Willow got into her car, waving as she pulled away, and Lou walked down the street, back to the bookshop. Happy as she was to have helped her friend, she hoped she hadn't missed her only chance to check Chandler's alibi in the process.

CHAPTER 17

When Lou returned to Whiskers and Words, she couldn't believe how good it felt to be home. One of the things she loved most about cold winter runs was the satisfaction she felt after, the deep-in-her-bones warmth that would surround her once she returned home.

The bookshop was toasty, a fire crackling in the corner. The older cats crowded around the hearth, lying in various loaf positions as close to the heat as they dared. The kitten pen was equally cozy. The remaining kittens had fallen asleep in one of the beds, creating an adorable pile. The cinnamon-scented pinecones Lou had placed around the shop made everything smell festive, punctuated by the spicy scent of the spruce coming from the Christmas tree in the corner.

Besides a few customers milling about, Olivia was the only one there.

"I sent them off to grab coffees," Olivia said, not needing Lou to voice her question about where her parents had gone. "How was the run? Fruitful?" She appraised each of the customers, making sure they weren't listening too closely.

Lou wrinkled her nose. "In some ways, but not the ones we'd hoped."

Olivia nodded along as she listened to Lou explain how she'd lost Chandler right away and hadn't been able to find him again, especially not after her pit stop at the garden shop. Lou lifted the bag full of gifts in a what-can-you-do? gesture.

"This is okay. It's fine." Olivia's eyes traveled over the ceiling as she processed the news. "Maybe Chandler wants a kitten too. We could get him in here to talk in the same way we're getting Marla to come. If she does." Olivia crossed her fingers.

Lou pulled in a deep breath. "I don't know. I've been thinking about that, and, if either of them is the murderer, I don't want them to adopt a kitten."

Olivia scoffed. "Don't let them actually *have* one, at least not until you find out whether they could've done it. But it'll get them in here, and then you can tell them that applicants must wait a certain number of days to buy yourself time. I mean, Marla's the wife of the deceased, which means she has to be on Easton's list, so I'm sure you could ask him, if you're really curious about her alibi." Olivia smirked, knowing Lou wouldn't want to do that.

"And let him know I'm even slightly involved in the case?" Lou wrinkled her nose. "I don't know." As she contemplated that idea, Lou paused. "Wait. Why are you saying *you*? Don't you want to be involved in this interrogation?"

Olivia's expression fell. "I do, sweetie, but I've gotta get going tomorrow."

The information settled over Lou like a rush of snow from a snowplow. Of course she'd known Olivia would leave at some point—heck, she'd spent the better part of last week wishing she would move on early—but now that they were back into their old rhythm, she didn't want her friend to leave.

"Are you sure you can't stay for a little while longer? If you have to check out of the inn, you can come stay here with me. Mom and Dad love their RV and totally don't mind sleeping there. Or Willow." Lou snapped her fingers. "She has a guest room, and I know she'd let you stay there for a few nights." Lou stopped herself just short of begging, knowing her tone was getting high and a little whiny.

Olivia smiled kindly, inclining her head toward Lou. "I'd love to stay, dear, but it's not up to me. I've got another signing in two days down in Oregon."

Lou blinked. "Oh, right. I forgot that you're on a book tour right now, not just visiting me."

"But I've had so much fun visiting," Olivia said. "I think once I'm not doing all of this traveling for press, I'll come back and take you up on that offer. This town is great for generating story ideas. I've already got my next book plot from all the events of this past week."

"There's very rarely a dull moment around here. And I thought moving from New York was going to be boring." Lou laughed. "I think this place keeps me on my toes even more."

"There's no disappearing into the background here, that's for sure." Olivia wet her lips.

Lunging forward, Lou pulled Olivia into a tight hug. "I'm going to miss you."

"Same here. And as exciting as it will be to visit Powell Books in Portland, I'd pick Whiskers and Words any day over that city block of books."

Lou warmed at the kind comment. "Thank you. Now I've just got to figure out how to ask Marla about her alibi if she comes in to look at the kittens." Lou chewed on her lip as she thought.

"Oh, I've got an idea for you there," Olivia said with a

sparkle in her eye. "That regular of yours, Forrest, the psychologist, came in while you were on the run. He doesn't know it, but he gave me a great idea."

Olivia left the following day around lunchtime. Lou still felt a little teary and sentimental after having to say goodbye to her friend. Which meant that, even though she was technically expecting her, Lou was caught off guard when Marla sauntered into the shop that afternoon. She'd shooed her parents out to have lunch at the bistro, so she was all alone in the bookstore. Lou wasn't sure if she was happy or worried about being alone to question Marla.

"Welcome to Whiskers and Words," Lou said after a beat, once she'd gotten over her surprise. "Marla, right?"

The woman's attention only landed on Lou for a second before it was pulled to the kitten pen. The way her face lit up at the sight of the kittens made Lou feel a little better about letting a murder suspect hold any of the sweet little creatures.

"So, these are the kittens?" Marla asked, moving to the edge of the pen and peering down at the playful group.

Lou walked over, shoving her hands in her pockets. "They're from two separate litters, but they're all between twelve and thirteen weeks old. That white one is Swan; Birdie and Frenchie are the tabbies; Turtle and Piper are the tortoiseshells. Goose, the black one with the white mustache, is actually already spoken for, but Goldie is the little orange girl in the center." Lou pointed out the cats as she said their names.

Marla squinted one eye while Lou talked.

"My dad named them after the 'Twelve Days of Christmas'

song, since there were twelve kittens," Lou explained, seeing her confusion.

"That's really cute." Marla chuckled.

Her fingers curled into fists as she watched the kittens. She reminded Lou of a little girl she saw standing outside the candy shop the other day who'd done the same thing instead of reaching out toward the candy she wanted.

"You can pick any of them up." Lou nodded toward the pen in encouragement. "Some are feistier than others, but we've handled them a ton. They're used to being picked up."

Marla's long fingers unfurled from their clenched position, and she wiggled them once before scooping up Goldie. The kitten automatically curled her tail and legs in toward her creamy-orange belly, and Marla set the little bundle in the crook of her arm like a baby.

Lou couldn't help but smile at the interaction. She gave Marla a moment to cuddle the kitten, but knew she didn't have much time and needed to get some information out of the woman while she was in the shop.

Olivia's plan played in Lou's brain as if it were a recording on repeat. *This might not be something they do on the force anymore, but back when I was a cop, we would sometimes give a suspect the impression that someone else connected to the case had pointed a finger at them. Forrest was reading some psychology book about paranoia, and I remembered the things people used to spill after hearing that someone else had accused them. Sometimes their reaction would be defensive enough that we knew to dig deeper into their alibi. Other times, they gave up information they'd been keeping from us to make themselves look better. Either way, I think it might work in this instance.*

The thing was, Lou was neither an ex-cop nor a psychologist. She hoped she could pull off the same results Olivia had mentioned.

"I'm so sorry about your husband, by the way." Lou picked at the hem of her sweater, her discomfort at having to bring up the subject audible in her crackly delivery of the apology. "I'm a widow too. It's hard to lose a loved one at any time of year, but Christmas is extra difficult."

Marla had been scratching Goldie behind the ears. At Lou's statement, her fingers froze in place.

Once a few seconds had passed, it became clear to Lou that Marla wasn't going to say anything, so Lou decided a direct question might be best. "Do the police have any idea who's responsible?"

"No." Marla shook her head once, like a door slamming shut.

Suddenly, Lou knew for sure she couldn't follow Olivia's plan. It might've worked for officers of the law who were already questioning someone, but she didn't feel comfortable implicating Marla, to her face, even if it was under the guise of what someone else said.

Switching gears, Lou said, "I heard someone in town say they thought it might be his business partner. The guy who's taking over the company now that he's gone."

Marla exhaled quickly through her nose in a sarcastic laugh. "Chandler? No, that guy wouldn't hurt a fly unless someone came after his family. Plus, he was one of the few people who actually liked my husband."

Lou's eyebrows rose. "Yeah?"

Smiling in that tight way that told Lou she wasn't amused by the conversation, Marla looked down at the cat. Goldie had fallen asleep in the crook of Marla's arm, her orange paws wrapped around the hand Marla had been petting her with. "I think this is the one I want. Do you have an application I can fill out?"

Lou wasn't surprised by Marla's pick. She'd come to love Goldie and her spunky personality. But she really couldn't let the kitten go until she knew for sure what Marla had been doing during the times her husband and Ferris were murdered.

"Absolutely," Lou said with a smile. "You can definitely fill out the paperwork today." Lou chewed on her lip for a moment. "But Dr. Romero has to approve all adoptions, so it'll take at least a day." As she said the words, Lou wasn't sure if that would buy her enough time, so she added, "Also, Goldie is still on watch with Dr. Romero. She had a little infection after her spaying surgery, and he just wants to do another checkup on her before he lets her go." Lou inwardly cringed, hoping Noah didn't mind her using him as an excuse to keep the kitten a few more days.

Marla faltered, having not expected the time constraints. "Okay, I don't mind waiting."

"You're free to use the table here to fill out the application." Lou motioned to the table where Sapphire was taking a nap on one of the fleece beds Noah and Marigold had sewn for the cats. As she passed Marla the application and a pencil, Lou wondered if she could get away with asking about Marla's schedule. But from the tight set to the woman's jaw and the irritated slant to her writing, Lou figured she'd pushed the woman too far already.

"Here you go." Marla slid the paper over to Lou a few minutes later. "Please let me know when she'll be ready."

"I will." Lou trained her eyes on Marla as she headed for the door.

Once she was gone, Lou texted Noah.

> I need to ask you something when you have a moment.

Thinking about Chandler's and Tom's alibis, Lou added another text after that.

> Also, if you get a chance, can you ask around and see if you can verify that Tom Rockwell was at Chandler's meeting with that plumber on the first? Thanks!

After those were sent, she picked up Goldie, scrunching her fingers into the kitten's soft fur. "Okay, girl. Now that I've bought us a few days, we've got to make sure your future owner didn't kill anyone."

The kitten purred, blissfully unaware of the drama surrounding her.

CHAPTER 18

The rest of the day went by in a sleepy Monday fog, literally. A frosty fog crept into Button, layering the town in a deep gray that seemed to push everyone home early. Given that their only plans that evening were to play board games after they returned from another play practice, Lou didn't mind the slower-than-normal afternoon in the bookshop.

She and her parents were about to retire upstairs for the evening when there was a knock on the bookshop front door. Noah stood just on the other side. His breath billowed around him in the cold.

Lou jogged over and unlocked the door, letting him inside.

"Sorry, I had to get Marigold over to Cassidy's. Now, what did you want to talk to me about?" He shoved his hands in his pockets as he bustled inside. "Are you having a plumbing problem?"

Lou glanced back at her parents. She didn't exactly want them to know what she was going to divulge to Noah. It wasn't that she couldn't trust them, but she didn't want them getting involved if she could help it.

Apparently, she didn't need to worry, however, because Caroline pointed up the stairs. "I think we'll head up, honey. We'll let you two chat alone."

Lou's mother didn't wink or anything suggestive to imply that she thought they needed their privacy, but Lou couldn't help but think of Olivia and the conclusion she'd first jumped to when she saw Lou and Noah talking.

"I'll see you up there soon. I just need to run something by Noah about the adoptions." Lou waved to her parents as they took the herd of shop cats along with them.

Lou turned back to Noah. She had to admit that Noah was handsome. She'd noticed that from the start. He had a way of calming her down that she'd never experienced with anyone else. And Olivia's comment about finding someone different from Ben stuck in her mind.

She wet her lips, aware she'd been staring at him for more than a second, and things were about to get awkward. "I, uh, need to run something by you," she said, eager to change the subject but worried about telling him what she'd done.

"But it's about the cats and not plumbers?" Noah asked, her two texts confusing him.

"Oh," she said. "The plumber is a different request. I'll get to that in a moment. First, I need to tell you that I lied to a potential adopter today."

Noah's deep-brown eyes focused on her in a way that made her sure he wouldn't judge her for anything that came out of her mouth.

"Marla Crawford came in earlier. She's interested in adopting Goldie." Lou paused, biting her lip.

"And you're not sure if you want to let her take one since

Easton hasn't found the killer yet," Noah said, showing he didn't need her to explain herself.

At that moment, Lou felt like hugging Noah. She wasn't sure if she would've done it before her talk with Olivia, and now she was self-conscious, but lunging forward and wrapping her arms around the man seemed too personal.

"Exactly," she said with a tired exhale. "But in order to keep her at bay until we—uh, Easton figures out if she's the killer, I need your help. I told her you had to approve all applications."

They'd started that practice because a person on the town's adoption ban list had tried to adopt one of the bookshop cats earlier that year. Noah knew the list and the people in the town well, so he worked as a second check.

"But she seemed quite motivated, and I'm not sure if that'll keep her at bay long enough, so I added that she'd gotten a tiny infection from her surgery, and you wanted to do one last examination before you gave her the green light to go home with someone." Lou grimaced as she rushed through her explanation.

Noah's mouth tugged into a grin. "You're getting too good at this."

"You mean, that works?" Lou asked in surprise.

"Totally." Noah dipped his chin. "I can even not be completely satisfied with my last exam if you need to hold her longer."

Lou felt relief wash over her. Having his support made her instantly feel better. "Thank you, Noah."

His gaze shifted over to the pen of sleeping kittens. "Anytime."

"There is one more thing you could help me with, before I explain the text about the plumber." Lou's eyes sparkled. "It has to do with Goose."

Noah listened, nodding along as she told him the plan. He smiled. "I'm in. Absolutely. I can take him tonight. Do you want to grab a carrier for him, and I can take him with me now?"

"Sure." She held up a finger and jogged to the back room where she kept the cat supplies. Plucking one of the small crates off the stack in the corner, Lou caught sight of the bag of purchases from the garden shop yesterday. "Oh!" she exclaimed, setting the cat carrier down for a moment.

Plucking two items from the gift haul, she opened the drawer where she kept fancy gift bags and wrapping paper, and twiddled her fingers until she found a Christmas bag that would fit the packages. Then she fluffed some tissue paper, so it sprung out the top and hurried back into the bookshop carrying the bag and a cat carrier.

"I have a cat carrier *and* a gift," she explained.

Noah's face lit up in surprise as he took in what she held. But Lou's heart constricted as his expression, just as quickly, dropped into a frown.

"Lou, I—I don't have a gift for you." He put up his hands in apology, as if he couldn't accept the gift if he didn't have something to give her in return.

Lou's lips parted. She'd created the exact awkward scenario Willow had been worried about with Easton, though it was worse because she and Noah weren't even dating. Shaking her head, Lou chuckled.

"Oh, no. It's for Goldie." Lou held the gift forward. "Your Goldie, not the cat Goldie." She hadn't realized the link between the cat and Noah's daughter until that moment.

Noah's entire body relaxed from the stiff posture it'd been held in. "Oh, good." His eyes flicked nervously over to Lou. "It's not that I ... I've just been so busy with the play this year and—"

Lou placed a hand on his arm and passed the gift bag over

to him. "You don't need to explain. I just saw it and thought of her." Lou held a hand up to her mouth and cupped it, as if she were telling a secret, as if they weren't the only two people in the bookshop. "It's a cool paper-star lamp. I thought it would be so cozy in her room, and I could picture her reading underneath it in the warm glow of light." Lou's cheeks heated as she admitted the next part. "I also couldn't decide between two colors, so I bought them both. I figured she could have one at your place and the other at Cassidy's." Lou bounced on her toes in anticipation as Noah peered into the bag.

A stunned silence hanging in between them.

"Lou, this is—" Noah started but broke off.

She didn't have more than a second's notice before he stepped forward and pulled her into a hug. The gift bag swung around behind them. But Lou didn't care. She sank into Noah's embrace. His strong arms wrapped around her, and he even tucked his head down, so it cradled hers, as if surrounding her just with his arms was not enough.

The ironic part of Lou's mind couldn't help but latch on to the fact that she definitely could've given in to her urge to hug him earlier. But then the relationship part of Lou's mind, that longed for connection, took over, and she couldn't help but analyze the true greatness of the hug she was receiving.

Lou squared her shoulders in an effort to compose herself as Noah pulled away. He grinned down at her.

"She's going to love this." He lifted the gift bag. "I don't know how you knew, but she'd just had a conversation with me the other day about how she wished she could have double of everything, so she didn't miss anything when she was at our different houses." Noah swallowed. "It broke my heart a little, but this is going to make her day."

Lou felt a few too many emotions to come up with anything

clever or profound to say. "I'm so glad," she finally croaked out. Desperate to break the awkwardness hanging in the air, Lou said, "Oh, did you have time to ask about Tom's alibi?"

"I did, actually," Noah said. "Dean said he was at the Rockwells' house that afternoon, and Tom was the one who met him there to let him in."

"*Just* let him in?" Lou narrowed her eyes.

Noah shook his head. "He said Tom stayed the whole time until he left around seven. That was why Tom wasn't at the lighting."

Lou was satisfied with that answer. "Thanks for doing that."

She helped Noah get Goose in the carrier, and then he was off. And Lou couldn't help but feel like the bookshop was just a little colder and emptier whenever he left.

THE NEXT MORNING, George was sitting inside the pen, surrounded by kittens, when she looked up at Bruce and wrinkled her nose.

"I don't see Goose. And Goldie's here, but her adoption profile isn't on the wall anymore," she said as she stroked the slim kitten. "Did someone adopt them?"

As much as George loved the cats, she'd yet to adopt one herself, saying she'd know when she met the one. Lou wasn't sure what she was waiting for, knowing she loved hanging out with the older cats and kittens alike. Plus, anyone who had eyes and a heart connected with the sweet Anne Mice, so whatever George was searching for in a cat was obviously different from most.

Bruce glanced down at the twentysomething. "Goose? Wait.

He was just here last night." He walked over to search the pen for the black kitten with the white mustache.

Having watched the whole interaction, from where she was going through her monthly numbers at the computer behind the desk, Lou poked her head over the counter. "Um, actually, Goose did get adopted last night. That's part of what Noah had to talk to me about," Lou said, trying not to linger on the sadness in her dad's expression. He'd really had a connection with Goose and was obviously sad to see him go. She pushed on. "And Goldie *is* spoken for. Marla Crawford came in yesterday and filled out paperwork. Noah just has to look over it, and he wanted to do a last exam before she goes to make sure she's all healed from her surgery." Lou inwardly congratulated herself, again, on the convincing lie.

Bruce watched his daughter. For a moment, it seemed like he might not have bought the excuse, but then he muttered something and walked off into the fantasy section. George and Caroline disappeared back there as well, and Lou distinctly heard whispering coming from the far corner of the shop.

Lou didn't think much of it until he and her mother came wandering over a little later once George had gone, their expressions as stiff as their posture. Their eyes shifted around the room, looking from Lou to the kitten pen. Noticing her parents' fidgety body language, Lou cocked an eyebrow in their direction as she looked over from the computer screen.

"What's up, you two?" she asked.

Bruce scratched at his cheek, messing with his mustache. "Uh, what makes you think something's up?" he asked with a hoarse chuckle.

Caroline shot him a glare before focusing her attention back on Lou. "Something *is* up, Bruce. We need to tell her the truth."

Lou rested her hands palms down on the counter, quite sure

she knew what was coming next. Her father would want to know who'd adopted Goose and if she could get him back. "What is it?" she asked, even though she was pretty sure she wasn't going to be able to help.

Bruce swallowed. "You need to take back the adoption application for Goldie."

Lou coughed in surprise. It wasn't about Goose. "Why?"

Caroline winced. "Lou, I'm so sorry. We didn't realize someone had adopted the cat."

Her parents were tense with worry, and a hint of sadness sat behind their eyes.

"Wait. Do you—is it because—you like her?" Lou asked, wondering how she'd missed the signs.

"Of course we like her." Bruce wrinkled his brow. "She's a fantastic kitten. They all are," Bruce said defensively as if it would be mad to suggest otherwise.

"I'm so sorry. I didn't realize." Lou tapped her fingers on the counter in front of her, wondering how she could get herself out of this.

"Realize what?" Caroline asked warily.

"That you've decided you want to add a cat companion to your lives. You know, I've heard cats can be quite happy living in an RV, especially if they have an adventurous disposition." Lou glanced over at the kittens. She wouldn't have picked out Goldie necessarily—the kitten was probably a little too feisty and troublesome to be contained in a small space like an RV— but she hadn't spent as much time with her as her parents had, so maybe they'd seen something in her that she hadn't.

Caroline started and stopped speaking three times before elbowing Bruce.

"It's not that, Lou." He tilted his head to one side. "Though, now that you mention it, a cat in the RV might not be a terrible idea."

Caroline aggressively cleared her throat.

Bruce got the hint. "Right. Well, the thing is that … don't you think you should really look into the people who are adopting these cats?"

Lou nodded. "Sure. I do. Noah does too."

"Yes, but *really* evaluate them," Caroline added. "I mean, how do you know they'll be a good fit for the kittens?"

Lou contemplated this. At that point, she'd helped many cats find forever homes through her bookshop. There had been a few that hadn't worked out, but in general, there was a feeling that helped her know they would be a good fit. She liked to make sure that the potential adopters spent some time with the cats so she could see how they interacted, but other than the case where the person had been part of a pet-selling ring, Lou had never gotten a bad vibe from anyone who'd wanted to adopt one of her foster cats.

"I don't know, Mom. They just click." As she said the word, Lou's brain did just that: clicked. If they didn't want Goldie for themselves, the only other reason they might not want the kitten to be adopted by Marla was… Lou's eyes widened, and she pointed an accusing finger at her parents. "You've been investigating the case behind my back. Haven't you?"

Bruce's cheeks turned a deep shade of pink, and Caroline muttered out a string of unintelligible excuses.

"You have," Lou said resolutely. "And you learned all about how Arthur was going to divorce her and leave her with nothing. The fact that she gets to keep his money now makes you think she's the one who killed him, and you don't want the kitten to go to a murderer." Lou crossed her arms in front of her body in triumph at her discovery.

But the confused scowls she was getting from her parents made her pause.

"Actually," Bruce said, dragging out the word as a self-satisfied smile tugged at the corners of his mouth. "We hadn't heard about that part."

Caroline cocked her head at her daughter. "We began suspecting her when we found out that she was the reason Arthur did the lights this year in the first place. Apparently, she pushed the man into volunteering and made sure he was the one who was putting up the lights." Caroline made an isn't-that-suspicious? expression.

"Don't forget that she lied about where she was between the hours of three and seven on the day of the tree lighting." Bruce held up a finger.

Lou blinked as she took it all in.

"Look who was also getting involved in the case." A goofy grin pulled across Bruce's face. "Seems someone couldn't take her own advice, huh?"

"Fine." Lou shuffled her feet at the admission. "I may have suspected her, and I may or may not have been asking around about her." At that moment, her hypocrisy wasn't the most important thing. Her parents had found out the piece about Marla that she was missing. "Wait, so she doesn't have an alibi for the time when Arthur was killed?"

"Not only does she not have an alibi," Bruce said, "but she lied about where she was." He cocked an eyebrow to punctuate his words.

Lou chewed on her lip. "How do you know? Where did you find this out?"

"George told us," Caroline supplied.

So that was what they'd been whispering about, Lou realized.

As if they were performing a practiced scene from a play,

Bruce took over the story. "Marla called George to help her install a new internet router, and when George stopped by, Marla wasn't at home."

"Which normally wouldn't be weird," Caroline said. "But then George heard Ruby say that when Marla told her about Arthur's murder, she said she was at home during that time."

Lou almost wanted to laugh at the he-said-she-said small-town gossip mill, and how her parents had become involved so quickly. But this was serious. She finally had the answer as to whether or not Marla had an alibi for her husband's murder. She didn't, and the fact that she'd lied to cover it up spoke volumes.

Bruce widened his eyes dramatically. "Which is implicating in and of itself, but paired with what you found out about her and Arthur's finances, it seems pretty clear she cannot have that kitten."

"Why do you think I told Marla that Goldie needed to stay here for a few more days for observation?" Lou asked rhetorically, shooting a knowing smile at her parents.

"I *thought* there was something more going on last night." Caroline chuckled.

Bruce waggled his eyebrows. "I mean, so did I. Just a different something."

"Dad!" Lou blinked at his brazen comment.

He checked with Caroline, as if wondering what he'd said that was so wrong. "What? I don't think I'm the only one who's noticed there's something between the two of you."

"There's not," Lou said through lightly clenched teeth. She felt all of sixteen again, being hassled by her parents when they found out she might have a crush on a boy.

Caroline reached out, placing a hand on Lou's arm. "You know, it would be okay if there was."

Lou softened.

"You're allowed to move on, honey," Caroline continued.

"I know." Lou pressed her lips into as much of a smile as she could muster to show her parents she was okay.

But before she could even think about her love life, she needed to find out who was going around committing murders in her small town.

CHAPTER 19

As much as Lou was loving having her parents stay with her, she was more than a little relieved when they left that afternoon to get the last-minute props, costumes, and scenery ready for the dress rehearsal of *A Christmas Carol* at the elementary school. Their insistence that they would be happy to see Lou move on and accept a new love in her life mixed with her own confusing feelings about Noah and had created a recipe for a wandering mind.

She'd spent the better part of the day spacing out as she thought through what it all meant, and couldn't ignore the interested gazes of her parents, as if they knew she was considering what they'd said.

Even if she was ready, she had no idea if Noah wanted a relationship again. He and Cassidy had only been divorced for two years. She'd felt a spark from him more than once, but what if he only saw her as a friend? Would trying to start something ruin the great friendship they'd built over the past year?

Try as she might to answer any of those questions, she only seemed to pile on more worries.

Desperate to shut off her mind, Lou pulled out a book and began reading. Between the snow piled up in small drifts on the sidewalks outside and the fire crackling in the hearth, Lou felt like a cozy Christmas romance was just what she needed.

So she sank deep into the soft couch and had descended equally into the beautiful story when Marigold came rushing into the shop looking downright frantic an hour before Lou closed. Her wide brown eyes locked on to Lou, and she raced over.

"Oh good. You're here." Marigold practically collapsed on the sofa next to Lou. "We have an emergency."

Lou's heart began racing, and she was just about to jump into action when Noah raced into the bookshop, breathing hard.

He held up a hand. "A hair emergency, not a regular emergency," he said, as if he knew his daughter would leave out key details.

Marigold nodded emphatically. Lou took in the state of the little girl. She was wearing a small velvet robe, slippers, and held something that seemed to be half swim cap, half gray wig: her Scrooge costume for the play.

"Mom's out of town today for business, and Daddy can't get it right. Can you help me, please?" Marigold held out a brush that Lou hadn't noticed was clutched in her small fingers, until then.

Lou blinked as she caught up. "Sure. What do I need to do here?" She glanced over at Noah, who opened his mouth, then closed it, looking completely lost.

"I need my hair in really tight French braids, so it'll fit under my bald cap," Marigold explained seriously.

Noah sighed. "I thought I had the hair stuff down when I

perfected the sleek ponytail, but I can't seem to get the braids tight enough," he explained.

Lou took the brush as proof she was taking on the job. "Tight braids? Coming up!"

Marigold let out a deep exhale, soaked in relief. She moved so her back faced Lou and she pulled the current hair tie from her dark locks. As Lou worked on her hair, she pulled information from Marigold, asking her if she was feeling better about remembering her lines, and how she felt the rehearsals had been going.

"So much better," Marigold reported. "I haven't forgotten a line since"—the little girl squinted, then turned to her father for confirmation—"last week. Right, Dad?"

"Yes," he confirmed. "She's been doing so much better since she had that practice session with your dad on Saturday."

"I'm so glad it helped." Securing the last braid, Lou surveyed her work. "Okay, I think we're ready. Hand over that bald cap, and let's see if it fits now."

Marigold passed her the cap, with wild, gray hair missing along the crown, mimicking an older man with a balding head. With Marigold's hair secured tightly to her scalp, the cap slipped right on.

Lou adjusted it a little to one side and then patted Marigold on the shoulders. "You're all set."

Marigold whirled around, enveloping Lou in the tightest hug. "Thank you."

Noah repeated his daughter's sentiments as Lou stood and walked them to the door.

"You're coming to the dress rehearsal, right?" Marigold tugged on Lou's arm.

She hadn't planned on going, the actual show being the next day, but she couldn't say no to the little girl.

"Of course." She assessed the state of the shop. "Let me just close up shop here, and I can come with you two."

Marigold latched on to Lou's hand so tight that she wasn't sure if the girl would ever let go. She must've been nervous, and even though Noah was there, not having her mom there, too, was probably affecting her more than she wanted to admit.

Together, they piled into Noah's truck and drove up to the elementary school.

MARIGOLD WAS WHISKED AWAY to get into makeup practically the second she stepped foot in the school. Noah stood with Lou for a minute, but he, too, was pulled away to help with a set-design emergency.

Lou felt out of place without a job. She moved to the back of the space, behind where the chairs would be set up for the audience tomorrow. It was then that her best friend came over, holding on to a small fern like it was a baby.

"Hey, stranger." Willow's expression lit up at the sight of Lou. "What are you doing here?"

Lou motioned to the diminutive Scrooge, taking the stage as they spoke. "The star invited me. I think she's a little nervous because Cassidy couldn't come tonight."

Willow pressed her lips together for a second to hide a grin. "Ah, gotcha."

They listened to the first scene for a few minutes.

But Lou couldn't get George's information about Marla's lie out of her mind. And while she didn't want to take advantage of the fact that her best friend was dating a detective, it also couldn't hurt to check in. They really hadn't talked a lot lately between Willow's busy schedule and Lou's visitors.

"How's Easton doing with the murder cases?" Lou tried to keep her voice light, letting Willow know she was just checking in.

Willow shrugged. "A little stumped, to be honest. Why?" She fixed her friend with a squinty side-eyed glare.

Lou glanced over her shoulder to make sure no one was close enough to hear what she was about to say. "I heard someone say that Marla lied about her alibi."

Willow's eyes went wide. "Wait. What?" Willow grabbed Lou's hand and pulled her into the supply closet where they could be alone.

"Marla Crawford," Lou repeated. "Arthur was going to divorce her, and he was laying the legal groundwork so she would get an excessively small percentage of their money. The only way she could get around it was if he died. She was the one who signed him up to do the Christmas lights, which were sabotaged, and she said she was home during the time he was killed, but George went to her house to set up a router, and she wasn't there." Lou took a breath. "Which means she doesn't have an alibi for the time her husband was killed. Granted, I don't know where she was when Ferris was killed, but the first part doesn't look good."

Instead of reacting to the surprising revelation, like Lou kind of hoped she would, Willow's frown only deepened.

"But she *does* have an alibi for Arthur's death. Easton confirmed it." Willow paced, pausing for a moment to make sure she was remembering correctly before doubling down with a nod. "Yes, I remember Easton saying that Marla was in a meeting with her lawyer, trying to see if there was anything she could do to protect herself financially during a divorce, when Arthur was killed."

"That's not what she told Ruby." Lou chewed on her lip. "Why would she lie?"

Willow cocked an eyebrow. "Maybe she didn't want the whole town to know she was seeking the advice of a lawyer."

Lou had to concede that point.

"And I would trust what she told the police over what Ruby heard," Willow said.

"Wait." Lou narrowed her eyes. "Easton told you about this?"

Willow wrinkled her nose. "Well … not exactly. I mean, he got a call from the station during dinner earlier this week, and he stepped into the other room. He's not as quiet as he thinks he is, so I caught his side of the conversation and pieced it together."

The information felt like a bucket of water dumped over the flames of Lou's investigation. "And if she wasn't the one to kill Arthur, she wouldn't have any reason to want Ferris dead either."

"Right," said Willow.

Lou knew she shouldn't be upset to learn that someone wasn't a murderer, but there had been so much evidence leading them to Marla.

"I think maybe we're back to Chandler, then." Lou wasn't sure if she was excited or dreading looking into him more.

But Willow stopped that train of thought in its tracks too. "He also has an alibi for Arthur's murder."

Lou blinked. "Are you sure?"

"That's the problem, actually," Willow explained. "Easton has a ton of alibis for people during Arthur's murder and almost none for Ferris's. He was muttering about it the other day. Chandler was in a client meeting during the whole window."

"Do you know who it was with?" Lou asked, skeptical.

"Because Robert said he swore he saw Chandler driving to the park."

Willow's eyes sparkled in the dim light of the closet. "Actually, I think I do know who his meeting was with. When I went to have lunch with Easton the other day, Julia was leaving the station. The woman is so chatty, she stopped me and told me she'd been there to give a statement to corroborate an alibi. And since we know she's not Marla's alibi, it would make sense she might be Chandler's."

Lou nodded. "That makes sense. Maybe I'll see if I can get her to confirm that today."

"I think that woman would tell you her social security number if you asked." Willow rolled her eyes. "All she does is chatter away during the practices. If your parents weren't helping, this would've been a complete disaster."

Lou was glad her parents' time was being well used.

Turning to Willow, Lou said, "Look, Willow. I know you and Easton are together now."

Willow tilted her head from side to side to show that she still wasn't sure where the two of them stood.

"And I don't want you to think that you have to feed me information about cases behind his back," Lou added. "So as much as I appreciate you telling me about these alibis, please know that I don't expect this to be an all-the-time thing. Thank you."

"I know, and you're welcome," Willow said. "Now let's get back out there."

They crept back into the main room, just in time, it seemed.

"Where's Willow?" Caroline was zigzagging through the room. "Ah, there you are," she said as she approached. "We found a place for that fern."

Willow followed Lou's mother with the plant, leaving Lou alone.

Pride glowed in Lou as she watched Marigold act. Noah stood off to the side, ready with her script in case she needed a line, but she didn't miss a beat. Caroline and Bruce spun around the place, helping with this and assisting with that.

About midway through, someone sidled up to Lou. She glanced over to find the same blonde woman she'd seen the last time she was there. The woman had a jacket slung over one arm and wore her purse over the other shoulder, like she'd just arrived.

"Which one is yours?" the woman asked.

"The two retirees." Lou chuckled, tipping her chin toward her parents.

The woman gasped and turned toward Lou. "You're Caro and Bru's daughter? The one that owns the bookshop in town?"

Lou coughed, startled by the woman's intense reaction.

"Omigosh, I feel like I know you already and that I owe you a boatload of thank-yous for loaning out your parents to me." She patted her forehead with the back of her hand, as if she were breaking into a sweat just thinking about what she would've had to do without their help.

The word "me" caught Lou's attention. "Julia, the director, right?" Lou guessed.

The blonde woman beamed and held out her hand. "It's such a pleasure. Your parents are just wonderful."

"I tend to think so," Lou said, shaking Julia's hand.

Lou couldn't believe her luck. She wouldn't even have to go searching for Julia. The woman who could verify Chandler's alibi was right there next to her.

"Julia, I forget who told me about it, but someone said you were meeting with A-Plus Electric the other week." Lou waited until she could see recognition flash over Julia's features before moving on. "I'm thinking of hiring them to add some shelf lighting at the bookshop," Lou lied. "Were you happy with their service?"

Julia nodded. Apparently, Willow was right about the woman being chatty, because she didn't even question that word would've gotten around about her meeting. She'd likely told a ton of people.

"I mean, they haven't been out to do the job yet, but our meeting went great. Chandler is really professional, and he was able to give us a really fair price," Julia explained.

"Oh, you met with Chandler, not Arthur?" Lou asked in mock surprise.

Julia grimaced. "Technically, I think our meeting with Chandler was, like, right when Arthur died."

Lou relaxed, glad Julia had walked right into the setup she'd given her. So Chandler had an alibi. And so did Tom. As nice as it was to take people off her suspect list, Lou was left with the very worrisome reality that she now had no suspects in the murders of Arthur and Ferris.

Rational thoughts won out, reminding Lou that the only reason she needed to be involved before was to make sure she wasn't sending an innocent kitten home with a murderer. If it wasn't Marla, she really didn't need to worry. She could leave it alone, let Easton solve the puzzle of the two connected murders.

Lou couldn't help but notice the fact that Julia had arrived late for her own production's dress rehearsal. She inwardly chuckled, the sight only solidifying Willow's complaints about the woman's ability as a director. Lou just hoped Julia would be on time for the final production tomorrow.

She was about to sidle away from the director when her

gaze caught on the purse still clutched to her side. Attached to the strap was a small leather rectangle. Lou's mouth dropped open as she recognized the item. She had one just like it sitting in that bag of lost-and-found junk from their investigation of the park for clues the first day Olivia arrived.

A chill washed over Lou's skin.

CHAPTER 20

Lou stared at the purse attachment, and the specific details came into focus. Technically, it wasn't *exactly* like the one they'd found in Button Memorial Park. The one Julia had attached to her purse was blue, and it was filled with something instead of being empty, like the one Lou had found.

"Julia, can I ask what this is?" Lou asked, touching the leather rectangle. She was surprised to find it rather heavy and dense.

Julia's eyes lit up. "Oh, this? It's a Bag Mag. A really powerful magnet that holds your bag up off the floor so it doesn't get all gross, especially in public restrooms."

The word magnet tickled something at the back of Lou's mind.

"And is that the only one you have?" she asked. All too late, Lou realized her question was too oddly specific, and Julia wrinkled her nose at her wording. "I mean, when I order some, should I get one, or do you carry multiple?" she asked, trying to save the situation.

Julia shrugged, immediately moving past her initial confusion at Lou's question. "It depends. They make great gifts, so you could grab multiple if you want. I have a stack in my closet just in case I ever need a last-minute gift. I also sell them, if you're interested." At this, Julia turned her full attention on Lou, looking at her like she was a sub sandwich after a fast.

"What colors do they come in?" Lou asked, hoping it didn't sound insincere when she added, "I really like rose gold."

She suppressed an involuntary shiver at the lie. It wasn't that she *didn't* like rose gold, it was just that she hadn't ever pictured herself saying anything of the sort. But the leather piece she'd found in the park had been rose gold.

Julia rolled her eyes. "I mean, I'd love to have a rose-gold one, but that's reserved for the top sellers. They're really hard to get."

"Top sellers? Are there any of those in Button?" Lou asked.

"A few, actually." Julia's expression went all glassy, like she was reliving one of her dreams. "Marla Crawford, Elise Rockwell, and Keeley Hoyt are our local top sellers."

"That's a lot in one town." Lou blinked in surprise.

Her mind went over the names. Marla, while the wife of one of the victims, was accounted for during his murder. Lou hadn't ever heard of Keeley Hoyt. But she *had* heard of Elise Rockwell, specifically in connection with her husband, Chandler.

Marla might be right, that Chandler liked Arthur, but what if someone who loved Chandler wasn't as accepting about the man?

Julia didn't seem to find the number of top sellers odd. "We're a very elite town. A lot of talent all in one place."

"Well, I think I need to talk to you about getting a few of these for Christmas gifts," Lou said. "It's a great idea."

"It really is. It's changed my life," Julia said without a hint of sarcasm. "The only thing that gets a little annoying is that the magnet is so strong, and every once in a while, I find myself stuck because the magnet has attached to a metal surface while I'm walking." She chuckled. "It's *that* powerful. Almost took my purse strap off once."

Lou wanted to laugh along with Julia, but her story had just brought to light why Lou's brain had pinged during all this talk of magnets. The metal fence running along the fields of Button Memorial Park next to the parking lot. There had been that rectangular magnet stuck to the fence where the opening was.

Now the empty leather rose-gold sheath made sense. If someone had been in a hurry, and they'd been rushing through that opening in the fence, and their Bag Mag had gotten caught on the metal fence post, they could've tried wrestling it free until it broke apart. It all made sense.

Except one thing.

Lou had seen Elise working at the Button Boutique just before she'd left to pick up the boughs from Ferris. Elise couldn't have killed him. And if he'd been trying to blackmail the killer, the person she was looking for had to be free during both times.

Lou's mind whirred throughout the last scene of the play. She applauded with the rest of the small audience, mostly made up by parents. Before she could leave, Julia jogged to the stage.

"Everyone. Can I have your attention, please?" Julia waited until the parents and children were quiet before saying, "I would just like to thank all of you so much for your help. The students did an amazing job, and we couldn't have done any of this without our fabulous volunteers. So let's give them all a round of applause."

The crowd clapped, a few letting out whoops of encouragement.

Once the sounds died down again, Julia said, "I've been reading a lot about how we can best be present in our children's lives, and I would love it if you joined me in turning off your phones tomorrow during the performance. My husband will be here taking pictures, and I'd be happy to email them to anyone who asks. But I think giving our kids our undivided focus is the very best gift we can give them around the holidays." She smiled sweetly, but Lou could tell that there was a fire behind her eyes. "Mrs. Ellis has kindly volunteered her classroom for use as a coatroom, and I thought it would be a great idea if we all left our phones in our jackets." She held up a hand. "Don't worry, we'll lock the door, so your purses and valuables will be safe. Thank you for your cooperation and for helping give our children the gift of our attention." Pressing her palms together, she kissed her thumbs and then mimed throwing the kiss out to the crowd, waving as she did so.

Lou used the opportunity to sneak out the door and walked the couple of blocks home. She couldn't help but think that Julia might not make a good director, but she'd have a pretty promising career in writing political speeches.

The fact that Lou had no remaining suspects in Arthur's and Ferris's deaths left her feeling almost as confused as Julia's ending speech.

As much as Lou wanted to call Easton and talk through the clues with him, she didn't want to bug the detective. After experiencing so much frustration when her parents and Olivia had dismissed her warnings not to get involved, she understood why Easton was always asking her to stay out of investigations.

But even though the murderer was still unclear to Lou, one

thing was for certain: it was safe to let Marla adopt Goldie. Sending a text to Noah, she told him Marla had been cleared, and she was going to call her with the green light, which she did right upon returning to Whiskers and Words.

Marla was ecstatic and said she'd come by tomorrow to pick up the kitten.

"I'll be here," Lou said, worried the dry, flat tone to her voice gave away the frustration she was feeling about not knowing where to look next.

Once she hung up with Marla, Lou figured she might check in with Olivia. The woman would want to know about the recent developments in the case, after all. And maybe she would be able to see something Lou couldn't.

Slumping onto the couch in the bookshop, Lou dialed her friend. A digital song rang out from the couch where Lou sat. She frowned as she rummaged through the couch cushions until she pulled out Olivia's phone.

She'd accidentally left it behind.

"Classic Olivia," Lou muttered to herself.

The bell on the front door jangled as Lou's parents returned from the dress rehearsal. While Lou had thought the performance had been great, she knew her parents would see the show through a more critical lens, and she was excited to hear their thoughts.

From the skip in their steps as they sauntered in, she didn't even need to ask. It was obvious that they were proud of what the students had done that afternoon. Lou was even prouder that her parents could have such a positive impact in a short amount of time.

"Should we go out to dinner to celebrate?" Lou asked.

Caroline nodded. "I think we should."

"But we need to be quick because it's Christmas PJ day," Bruce said, cocking an eyebrow at Caroline as if he was disappointed with her for forgetting.

That was right. They were supposed to go shopping for the matching pajamas they would wear on Christmas Day as they opened presents in the morning. Lou had so many Christmas PJs that she had a one in, one out policy. Each year now, she had to get rid of an old pair when she bought the new one. But it was a family tradition, and she loved cozy pajamas as much as the next person, so she wasn't going to complain.

Scoffing, Caroline said, "Of course I remembered about Christmas pajamas. It's on the calendar." The smirk on her lips told Lou and Bruce something different, however, and they all suppressed smiles.

"Hey, Mom," Lou asked as nonchalantly as she could. "The other day when you went into the boutique to shop, was Elise working, or was it Heather?"

Lou had seen Elise right before she'd left to meet Ferris, but what if the woman had just started her shift? She could've killed Ferris and then gone straight to work.

Caroline paused for a moment as she thought. "I can't remember her name, but she had blonde hair."

Heather had dark brown hair. Elise, however, was blonde. Lou let the small bit of hope sink back into disappointment. Elise couldn't have killed Ferris.

"Whose is that?" Bruce asked, studying the phone in the black case that Lou held, so different from her sage green case.

"Olivia's," Lou scoffed. "She left it here." Lou walked over to the register counter and stashed the phone in the drawer for safekeeping. "I'll call the hotel she's staying at and let them know she left it behind."

With that, Lou and her parents bustled out into the frosty

evening to go to dinner, celebrating a successful dress rehearsal. But even though Lou felt happy as she savored her time with her parents, she couldn't help the feeling that she was missing something that tickled the back of her mind the rest of the night.

CHAPTER 21

The next morning was hopping for a Wednesday. Word must've finally gotten around town about the kittens because Lou and her parents adopted out all the remaining little ones before lunchtime.

Marla came to pick up Goldie that afternoon as well. After Lou privately explained why she was no longer a suspect, her parents consented to let the little orange kitten go with the new widow.

"She's rare, you know," Bruce said to Marla as she situated Goldie in the new travel carrier she'd bought for the kitten.

Marla blinked over at him.

"Most orange cats are males," Bruce clarified. "An orange female tabby like her, she's rare."

Marla nodded seriously, showing Bruce she understood. "I will treat her as such. Thank you for letting me know." And with that, she and Goldie had slipped out the front door and into the mid-December afternoon.

Because of the busyness, Lou didn't remember about Olivia's phone until after her parents had already left to set up for the final performance of *A Christmas Carol*. She opened the drawer looking for a sticky note to write herself a reminder to buy more cat litter, and Olivia's black phone stared back at her from the bottom of the drawer.

Right. She needed to call Olivia and let her know she'd left it behind. Lou needed to get going if she was going to make it in time for the play at the elementary school. But calling the hotel wouldn't take more than a minute, and Lou had already forgotten the phone once. She didn't want to chance it falling by the wayside again.

Locating her own phone, Lou pulled up the number of the hotel Olivia said she'd be staying at in Portland.

"Sentinel. How can I help you?" The male concierge on the other end of the line sounded chipper.

"Hi. Yes, I need to leave a message for one of your guests," Lou said, watching as the older shop cats came out from their napping places, seeming to realize they had the bookshop to themselves once more now that all the kittens were gone.

"Sure thing. Can I get the name of the guest you'd like to contact?"

"Olivia Queen," Lou answered. "I just need her to know that she left her phone with me. You can tell her the message is from Lou. She'll know what it's about."

The sound of fingers clacking against computer keys rang through the phone as Lou waited. Then there was a click of a tongue.

"I'm so sorry. Mrs. Queen never checked in," the concierge said.

Lou's whole body went hot and cold. "What?" She choked out the word. "She should've been there on Monday the twelfth."

"She never arrived," he added, his tone lilting up at the end in question, probably wondering what Lou didn't understand about what he was saying.

Lou thanked the man and hung up the call. If Olivia never arrived in Portland, where had she gone?

Lou took three deep breaths before she dialed Olivia's husband. There was probably a perfectly good explanation. Lou paced as she held the phone to her ear. She wasn't sure if Chuck would even answer given that he wasn't much better at keeping a cell phone on him than Olivia was, but she had to hope.

"Lou! How are you?" His goofy voice spilled through the line, sounding way warmer than Lou had any right to feel. The chill that had washed over her after her call with the hotel made her feel like ice dunked in a steaming cup of tea.

She relaxed a little. If Chuck was so chipper, maybe there really wasn't a problem. Olivia had ditched stops on her tour in the past. Maybe she decided she wanted to get home earlier so she could be with Chuck.

"I'm glad you called," he said. The noise fell away around him as if he'd stepped out of the room. "Livy texted me the other day, but I didn't get it right away. I tried calling her back, but she must've misplaced her phone again, and I'm not getting through."

"Yep. I found it in the cushions of one of my couches." Lou let out a dry laugh that felt like it cut her throat.

"Well, tell her I'm good out here, and she should definitely stay with you for the holidays," he said.

"What do you mean?" Lou asked, her voice cold and robotic.

"She sent me a message saying she was thinking of heading back to stay with you for the holidays instead of flying back home after Portland." He chuckled. "I knew it was going to be hard for her to leave your place in general, so I expected as much. Tell her not to worry about me."

Lou's fingers shook. She swallowed. "Right." Lou laughed robotically once more. "Okay, I'll let her know. Thanks, Chuck."

Lou hung up the phone and stood there. Guilt settled over her at lying to Chuck, but she couldn't be the one to break the news to him that Olivia wasn't with her.

Plus, it was just like Olivia to disappear without telling anyone what she was doing. It didn't necessarily mean something was wrong. If Olivia had texted Chuck that she wanted to stay, she was probably just hiding out in an inn somewhere in Button and would show up tonight, pretending to have come back after her Portland signing. She knew Lou hated it when she skipped out on her signings.

That all made sense, and Lou wished it could help with the worry gnawing at her gut, but somewhere deep down in her heart she worried this was the one time Olivia hadn't just been forgetful or flaky. The woman had been openly asking about Arthur and Ferris during her book signing. Any one of the guests they'd had that night could've been the one to spread the word that Olivia was interested in the case.

And by killing Ferris, the murderer had already proven that they were willing to kill to keep their secret safe.

A chill wound around Lou, and she tried calling Easton. It went straight to voicemail. She stamped her foot. Willow's phone did the same, as did her parents' and Noah's. That was right. They were all at the play, where she should be. She could just picture them all leaving their bags and jackets in the classroom at Julia's urging.

But how could Easton cut himself off from work like that? What if the station needed him? There had to be someone on call, someone she could talk to. Chewing on her lip, Lou thought of the only person sour enough, Scrooge-like enough not to be interested in attending the town production.

"Detective Anderson," Roy answered warily after Lou dialed his desk phone.

Lou wondered if the man recognized her number from the last case they'd crossed paths on. She hoped he hadn't, since those hadn't necessarily been positive interactions.

"Detective Anderson, this is Louisa Henry. I own the bookshop in town." She waited, hope hanging in the thick silence.

"I know who you are, Lou." His tone was flat. "Why are you calling me?"

Lou steeled her resolve, then said, "I think someone is missing, and Easton, along with everyone else I know, is at the elementary school right now watching the play, so I can't get ahold of them."

"Who is it that you think is missing?" the detective asked.

Despite his uninterested tone, he'd asked a question instead of hanging up on her. That was something.

"My friend, Olivia Queen. She was supposed to go to Portland for another book signing two days ago. She's an author. She's the author who did the signing at my shop last week, actually." Lou closed her eyes. She knew she was rambling. Detective Anderson had that effect on her. She paused for a beat to calm herself. "I just called to let the hotel know she left her cell phone here. She does that kind of stuff all the time, so I didn't think anything of it until I talked to the hotel, and she never checked in. Her husband hasn't heard from her either."

"Why doesn't her husband file a missing persons report, then?" Detective Anderson sounded tired.

"Well ... because I didn't tell him she's missing. He thinks she skipped out on her signing to stay in town with me. I didn't want to worry him until I knew for sure she's lost."

"But you're willing to bug me?" A long, tired sigh slid through the phone. "Look, you can come file a missing persons report, but I would suggest you're sure before you do that. Have you followed her tracks? Trailed where she was last? That might be a good place to start."

"That's actually a really helpful suggestion," Lou said. "Thank you. I will."

He snorted. "Thanks for sounding so surprised." He didn't even wait for Lou to say anything more, hanging up right after that.

Lou wasted no time bundling herself into her car and heading for the Button Inn.

The festive decorations gave Lou a warm feeling she had no business experiencing in the light of such a terrifying mission. Besides the large Christmas tree sitting in the lobby, adorned with red bows and glittering gold ornaments, lighted garlands ran along the crown molding and up the banister. Christmas music flowed through speakers—probably hidden by garland —creating a cheery atmosphere.

"What can I help you with?" Lou didn't recognize the woman standing behind the counter, but that didn't surprise her. She was still getting to know people in town after a year.

"Hi." Lou pulled her lips into her most endearing smile. "This might be a weird request, but I'm wondering if you, or any of your colleagues, might have information about a woman who recently stayed here. Her name is Olivia Queen."

At the name, the woman's eyes lit up. "Olivia? Sure. She was lovely." The woman pulled out a copy of Olivia's latest release. A red bookmark showed that she'd already gotten more than halfway through. "When she told me she was an author, I just had to try out her book. It's so good."

"She's a talented writer," Lou agreed. "And she's also a great escape artist. I can't seem to find her." Lou tried to make that sound the least alarming as possible. If Olivia really was just playing hooky with her responsibilities, Lou didn't want to get half the town worked up about it, only to have it fizzle into something not that bad. "Do you remember what she did on the day she checked out?"

"Sure." The woman nodded.

Lou's heart soared. "You do?"

"She said she was going to grab something to eat before she hit the road, and she asked if there was a good sandwich shop around. I sent her to Hoagies." The woman shrugged.

"Thank you!" Lou said, hopeful for the first time since she talked to that concierge. She jogged out to her car with a skip in her step.

Hoagies was a sub shop on Spool Avenue next to the pet shop. Because it was close to Willow's house, it was her go-to dinner or lunch spot whenever she was working in the barn and lost track of time, forgetting to eat—which was often. Lou had only ever seen one man working behind the counter, and she was sure he had a real name, but everyone just called him Hoagie.

One might expect a man named Hoagie to be wearing a too-small T-shirt, be sporting a potbelly, and have a gravelly voice. Lou had when she'd first heard the name. But Button's Hoagie was Mayor Teller Edwards's brother. He was just as small and quiet as the town's figurehead. Lou loved that after every topping someone ordered on their sandwich, Hoagie would nod once and say "lovely" as he was adding it to their sandwich.

The place always smelled like a hug of freshly baked bread, with just a hint of onions in the background. Being the late afternoon, Hoagie's lunch rush had passed, and he was keeping busy slicing very thin pieces of some sort of meat.

"Louisa, how lovely to see you! What can I get started?" He grabbed a piece of parchment paper from a precut stack and set it on the long counter that ran in front of him. Lifting the glass top so he could access the toppings, Hoagie's attention landed on Lou.

"Oh, I'm so sorry. I'm actually not here to eat." Lou winced apologetically. "I have a question for you."

Hoagie blinked in question, lowering the cover back over the refrigerated ingredients to keep them out of the open air. "Ask away," he said with a smile.

She described Olivia and asked if he remembered her coming in the other day for a sandwich.

Hoagie nodded once. "I do. She got an Italian with extra oil and vinegar. Great sandwich."

Lou chewed on her lip. "Did she say anything or do anything odd? I'm trying to solve a little mystery surrounding her movements that day."

Hoagie's thin lips pressed into a thoughtful line, and he tipped his head to one side. "She was rather chatty at first, and then I fear I said something wrong because she was fairly quiet after that."

"Do you remember what you said?" Lou wanted to lean forward on the counter but knew the glass partition was there for a reason.

Hoagie nodded once again. "Absolutely. I remember because she repeated it a few times. I got a big delivery of ingredients while she was here. She was surprised at the amount of stuff I received, and she asked if I had to unload it all myself. I told her she didn't need to worry about me. On delivery days, my wife and I divide and conquer to get the task done. She said 'divide and conquer' a few times and paced around while I finished making her sandwich."

A block of ice sat in Lou's stomach.

A block of ice with a very large light bulb frozen inside.

Because at that moment, Lou knew who had killed Arthur and Ferris, and she was pretty sure Olivia had figured it out two days before her.

Chandler Rockwell had an alibi for the time of Arthur's death. Elise Rockwell had an alibi for Ferris's death. But what if the married couple worked together? What if Elise, upset that Arthur wasn't actually going to step down and let her husband take over the business, had gone to get Arthur out of the way? If Ferris had seen her, as it seemed he had the night of the tree lighting, and tried to blackmail the Rockwells, Chandler might've taken him out to protect his wife. Hadn't Marla said as much? *That guy wouldn't hurt a fly unless someone came after his family.*

Ferris had, and he'd paid the price.

"Did she say anything else?" Lou asked, trying not to sound frantic.

Hoagie stared out the window for a moment as he seemed to find the right words. "She wanted to know where the Rockwells lived."

Lou wanted to close her eyes in defeat.

"I told her they're out in the neighborhood by Button Lake. You can't miss 'em because they usually have at least one A-Plus Electric van parked on the street near their house."

A groan built in Lou's throat, but fear constricted it from coming out. That wasn't good. Instead of going to the police, Olivia had gone to the home of the people she suspected had killed Arthur and Ferris.

Lou thanked Hoagie and raced out the door. Once in her car, she drove toward Button Lake, following Olivia's footsteps. She just hoped they weren't her last.

CHAPTER 22

Lou gripped the steering wheel as she drove. The sun was moving lower in the sky, like a ticking clock. It would be much harder to find Olivia in the dark. Desperate, she dialed the same number she'd called last.

"Detective Anderson," Roy answered, sounding just as *cheery* as before.

"I need you to meet me at Chandler and Elise Rockwell's home. I think they might've killed Arthur and Ferris, and I think Olivia realized it two days ago." Lou winced as she missed a stop sign.

"What?" Roy asked, his impatience giving the question the sharp edges of a scolding.

Making a split-second decision as she drove down Binding Street, Lou wrenched her steering wheel to the left and screeched to a halt in the parking lot of the Button Police Department.

"I'm outside the station. *Please* come out and drive with me to the Rockwells' house. I'll explain everything while I drive." Lou's voice shook as she pleaded with him.

"Tampering with an investigation is against the law, Mrs. Henry," Roy said before the line went dead.

Lou sat frozen for a moment, unsure what to do next. That wasn't completely true. She knew she had to go to the Rockwells' house and see if there were any signs that Olivia had been there. But she couldn't just go alone.

She needed Easton.

As much as she didn't want to interrupt Marigold's performance, Easton was her only hope. She would have to go to the play and bring him to search the Rockwells' home with her. This was life or death.

The word death, never pleasant, sent a wave of nausea over Lou. Oh, how Lou hoped Olivia was okay. She scolded herself for getting complacent. Ferris's death proved that Arthur's killer, or her husband, was willing to do anything to silence those who threatened them. And Olivia had done just that. Lou should've made sure the woman had left town safely.

Putting her car into reverse, Lou was about to back out of the parking spot and drive to the elementary when her passenger door opened. Detective Roy Anderson slid into the passenger seat.

Lou's mouth opened but nothing came out.

He held up a finger, continuing to look forward. "Tell me, in detail, why you think Chandler and Elise Rockwell are guilty." Pulling the seat belt across his chest, he buckled it with a snick that sounded so loud in the quiet car.

Knowing she would think better if she had a job to do, Lou reversed. "Okay," she said, putting the car into drive and heading for Button Lake. "Arthur Crawford was killed when he was electrocuted by Christmas light wires that had been intentionally stripped in multiple places. Someone removed the safety lock he'd put on the transformer while he was working. The locks they use for their tagout system have individual keys, but companies will often buy locks that open with a specific set of keys, so any of their employees can unlock them, in a bind. The killer either needed to be an electrician with A-Plus or know enough about the business to have access to one of those keys."

Lou's gaze flicked over to the detective as she drove. He nodded once, proving he'd also heard that information. Even though Easton was the detective leading the investigation, Button was a small town, and Lou was sure Easton was pooling all the station's resources into these cases.

She continued. "Arthur was supposed to step down, leaving the running of the company to Chandler. Robert Gavino told me that Arthur and Chandler had a meeting the day before Arthur died during which Arthur told Chandler he wasn't leaving. But Chandler was in a meeting with Julia Flanagan during the window of time Arthur was electrocuted."

Roy frowned but confirmed that statement.

"Elise Rockwell doesn't have an alibi. Robert Gavino saw someone driving Chandler's truck toward Button Memorial Park during that window. If it wasn't Chandler, it had to be Elise."

Lou immediately knew she'd made a mistake by making such a definitive statement because Roy pulled in a breath like he was about to correct her.

She held up a finger. "I have further proof. Tom Rockwell also has an alibi for the time of Arthur's death because he had to go meet the plumber at his son's house because Chandler's meeting went long, and Elise wasn't able to."

Roy's nostrils flared, but he stayed silent.

Lou took it as a sign to continue, but she also knew she needed to speed things up. Not only was she worried Detective Anderson might lose interest in her theory at any moment, but she was pulling up to the Button Lake neighborhood.

"I think Elise, the wife of an electrician, who was driving her husband's truck, which held all the tools she would need to pull off the murder, electrocuted Arthur Crawford."

Lou didn't mention the fact that she thought Elise's rose-gold top-seller purse magnet had gotten caught on the fence as she fled the scene of the crime, but she kept it in her back pocket in case she needed it.

"Ferris Howe must've seen her. Instead of going to the police with the information, he tried to blackmail the Rockwells for money. Chandler Rockwell killed him the following day while Elise was working at the Button Boutique. That's why nothing made sense about people's alibis. Two different people killed the two victims."

Lou swallowed as she spotted an A-Plus Electric van parked in front of a pretty cream-colored house to her right. She pointed out the black rental car Olivia had been driving around during her stay. It was parked on the other side of the street a few houses down.

"And there's my friend's car. She was supposed to leave for another signing in Portland on Monday, but she never made it. I think she figured this out before me and went to..." Lou opened her palms, grasping for a reason Olivia would've come to the house. "I don't know what she thought she was going to do. But she's in trouble, and we need to get into that house to save her."

Lou pulled her car off to the side of the road, turning to face Detective Anderson once she'd put it in park.

His eyes flicked from left to right as he processed. Lou's heart was in her throat.

"A warrant's going to take time. We can't just rush in there and arrest them." Even though Roy's tone was brisk, and his expression contorted into a scowl, Lou felt like hugging him.

He believed her.

"You don't have to arrest them, do you? Can't you bring them in for questioning? You can hold them for a while before having to charge them, right?" She tried to remember what Easton had told her about the time limits surrounding that law.

Pausing for a moment, Roy said, "Okay."

Lou turned off her car and moved to unbuckle her seat belt.

Roy held out a hand. "Oh, no you don't."

Lou glanced over at him in question.

"You do not need to be involved in me bringing them in. There's only one of them home, anyway." Roy motioned to the driveway where a silver hatchback sat in front of the garage.

"But Olivia might—" Lou started, reaching out toward the house.

"Let me go up there and look around. I will call some other officers for backup." He held her with his gaze as if he wished he could lock her in place.

He'd listened to her and he seemed to believe her. Lou needed to trust the detective. Leaning back in the seat, she said, "Fine."

Instead of getting out and going to the house, like Lou wanted him to, Detective Anderson pulled out his phone. Lou wanted action, not phone calls. She curled her fingers into fists to vent her frustration but knew complaining more to the detective wouldn't help her.

"Hi, Chandler. It's Detective Anderson from the Button Police Department." Roy paused for a second. "Yes, everything's fine. I was just wondering if you wouldn't mind coming in for questioning as soon as you can." Roy listened. "I understand you already gave a statement to Detective West. We just have a few more questions for you and your wife." Another pause. "Elise too. Yes. Okay. I will see you at the station in thirty minutes, then." Roy hung up the call.

Lou reached for the ignition. "So I need to drop you off at the st—"

But Roy cut her off, his hand shooting out to stop her from starting the car. His gaze was locked on the Rockwells' front door. Lou watched, too, realizing the detective might be onto something.

It seemed like minutes that they waited. But nothing happened.

Roy stayed poised in his seat, hand resting on his seat-belt buckle as if it were his firearm, and he was ready to draw it at any moment.

The front door swung open. Elise Rockwell raced out, clutching a cell phone to her ear. She glanced right and left before jogging toward her car parked in the driveway. Lou couldn't tell what she was saying, but her movements were frantic.

Roy unclipped, opening the passenger-side door at the same time. "Call Reynolds," he barked at Lou. "Tell him I need backup at the Rockwell place now. And tell him to get over to A-Plus Electric. We need Chandler Rockwell at the station."

Lou fumbled with her phone, trying to call the station while still observing what was happening out her windshield.

"Button Police Department," the ornery Officer Reynolds answered, punctuating the greeting with a nice, long yawn.

"Officer Reynolds, Detective Anderson says he needs backup at the Rockwell house immediately. He also says to send a unit to A-Plus Electric. He wants Chandler Rockwell in the station stat for questioning," Lou barked out the orders.

She hung up the call before Reynolds could hassle her, ask who it was, or ask why she was calling in orders for the detective.

Meanwhile, Anderson strode over to Elise, catching her just as she opened the door to her car and was about to climb in. It was like Lou was watching a silent movie. Roy said something, his right hand close to the gun she knew he kept in a hip holster under his jacket. Elise's eyes darted right and left.

Then she crumpled to the ground, hands up, breaking into a silent fit of sobs.

Lou's shoulders sank forward in relief, then immediately jumped in surprise as a Button PD cruiser tore past her car and screeched to a halt in front of the Rockwells' driveway.

Reynolds had listened, Lou realized with a surge of hope. She just had to believe another cruiser was pulling up in front of A-Plus Electric at that very moment, bringing Chandler Rockwell in as well.

Still looking like a movie on mute, Detective Anderson ordered the two officers around. One stood next to Elise as Roy helped her up off the ground, letting her sit in her car that was still open. The cruiser was parked behind her, so it wasn't like she could escape even if she wanted to. By the way she'd reacted to seeing the detective, however, it looked like she knew she'd been caught.

A few minutes later, another cruiser pulled up, and Chandler Rockwell spilled out, rushing for his wife. Every officer on the scene froze, at the ready as Chandler pulled his wife into a hug. The officers relaxed as the couple embraced, tears running down their cheeks. Detective Anderson gave them a moment, but then he pulled the two of them aside to ask them a question. The Rockwells shook their heads in tandem.

To Lou's surprise, Roy looked directly at her car and waved her over.

She stumbled out of the car and rushed to him.

"Lou, what's the name of your missing person?" Detective Anderson asked as she approached.

"Olivia Queen," Lou choked out, the combination of nerves and the cold air hitting her lungs making Olivia's name sound like a wheezing breath.

"Are you sure you have no information about the where-abouts of a woman named Olivia Queen?" The detective's voice growled with frustration. Lou wasn't sure if that emotion was directed at her or the criminals, but she didn't care. It had sounded intimidating, and that was all that mattered.

Intimidating or not, Chandler frowned and said, "Who?"

Desperate, Lou looked at Elise, but she blinked in the same confused manner. "I don't know who that is."

Not only was that not the answer Lou had been hoping for, but it also proved that neither of them were big readers. Olivia's name was a household staple for anyone who stepped foot in a bookstore in the last decade.

Roy turned toward Lou and leaned backward, as if to say, "What do you want me to do now?"

Grasping at anything else, Lou pulled up a picture of Olivia on her phone and shoved it in their faces. "This is her. Have you seen this woman?"

Elise and Chandler glanced at the phone. They shook their heads again. And while Lou wasn't a cop with lie-detection training, the couple didn't check with each other, and she didn't see a hint of recognition flit across their features.

"That's her car." She pointed across the street. "If they didn't hurt her. Why is her car still parked there?" Lou asked, her tone getting more high-pitched as her desperation rose.

"Look, we've already admitted what we did," Chandler said, wrapping an arm around his wife. "Why would we lie about something else? We don't know where your friend is."

Lou's heart sank. If that was the truth, where was Olivia?

CHAPTER 23

Discouraged, Lou slumped to the curb next to the Rockwells' house and let her head rest in her hands.

A hand landed on Lou's shoulder, tentative and awkward. She glanced up to see Detective Roy Anderson standing next to her.

He grimaced, which Lou wasn't sure was more about the situation or the fact that he was touching her, and said, "Look, if you really think she might be here, we can call the judge and see if we can get a rushed search warrant for their property."

Tears pooled in Lou's eyes. "Please." Lou knew it didn't make a lot of sense. The Rockwells were already caught. They'd already murdered two people. Why wouldn't they admit to kidnapping?

Lou's stomach was in knots as she hoped beyond measure it was *just* kidnapping.

Roy walked away, pulling out his phone and talking quickly to someone on the other end of the line. Lou stayed put, not caring that she was freezing or that she couldn't feel her toes anymore. The sun was setting, which she knew it would only make searching harder.

At some indeterminate time later—though it wasn't yet fully dark—a Button Police SUV pulled up to the scene. Easton got out of the passenger side, holding a few folded papers in one hand. Lou hoped one of those was the search warrant Roy had mentioned. But Easton wasn't the only one who got out of the car. Another officer slid out of the driver's seat and stopped at the door behind him.

Four paws hit the cold pavement a moment later. It was then that Lou noticed the words K9 Unit printed on the side of the SUV.

"Officer Peanut Butter," Lou whispered in joyful surprise, remembering the police dog from the Jingle Bell Run.

Officer Brenner walked Officer Peanut Butter over to the scene. Detective Anderson stopped him, pointing to Olivia's abandoned rental car and then around the Rockwells' home. Lou's heart soared with the last desperate threads of hope as the dog went to work, smelling the car's handle first before being led around the property.

The pair disappeared behind the house, and Lou got to her feet, waiting.

A few rapid barks rang out in the frigid evening air.

Lou let out a sob of relief. Detective Anderson glanced over, his eyes meeting with hers. He nodded, and they raced into the Rockwells' backyard. They found Officer Peanut Butter sitting in front of a green garden shed.

Lou raced over, along with Roy and Easton.

"We need bolt cutters over here," Easton called, cutting open the lock as soon as they were brought over.

Lou tried to give them space, but she couldn't help but rush forward and try to peer inside the shed as Roy pulled the double doors toward them. There was a lawn mower and a few rakes and brooms leaning up against the side. A portable heater glowed orange in one corner.

And lying on the floor, on a bag of top soil, was Olivia.

Lou couldn't seem to breathe for the moments before the woman stirred, turning to blink up at the light. Her face was pale, and her whole body shivered.

"Olivia, I'm so glad you're okay." She raced forward to pull the woman into a hug.

Her fingers were like ice as Lou grabbed her hand and helped her to her feet.

"Let's get you to a warm car," Lou said, leading her friend back toward the street.

"Call an ambulance," Easton ordered Peanut Butter's handler as he and Roy followed.

They waited until Olivia was warming up inside a cop car with Officer Reynolds and a bottle of water before Roy turned back toward Chandler and Elise Rockwell.

"How do you explain this?" he growled out the question.

"I've never seen that woman before." Elise's eyes were wide, like someone who just watched a magician pull a rabbit out of a hat. "I don't know how she got into the shed."

The humming of an electric car window stole everyone's attention, and they looked to see Olivia peering out the opening, Officer Reynolds's finger pressing down on the open button.

"They didn't kidnap me," Olivia croaked out. "I was snooping around their place when they came home, and I hid in the shed."

At that, Elise's eyes widened. "Chandler, do you remember when the garden shed door was open the other day?"

Chandler rubbed at his neck. "Yeah, I closed it and locked it."

"Trapping me inside," Olivia said.

"And your phone was at my place, so you couldn't call anyone," Lou said, tying up the last loose end.

Olivia cringed in a nonverbal apology. "I didn't realize it until I was already stuck in there."

"You could've called out for help," Roy said.

"And risk one of the two *murderers* hearing me and finding me in their shed because I'd been trying to find evidence they were *murderers*?" Between the sarcasm lacing her tone, the emphasis she put on the word murderers any time she used it, and the way she cocked her head to one side as she said it all, put Roy in his place.

He nodded in concession.

Olivia took another sip of her water, and then she turned her attention to Lou. "I knew you would figure it out and come looking for me. I just knew it." She smiled at her friend. "And here you are."

"But it could've taken me too long," Lou scoffed. "I mean, it took me two days longer than you, as it was. What was your plan?"

Olivia snorted as if she couldn't believe that Lou had such little faith in her. "I found that space heater in the shed, and I'd just stopped at Hoagie's, so I had a full sub sandwich in my purse and a bottle of water. I was rationing it out." Her face tightened. "Though someone's going to need to be very careful around the bucket in the back of that shed."

Lou couldn't help but laugh at the comment. "I wouldn't have figured it out without you."

"Sure you would've." Olivia winked, showing her she had

all the confidence in the world in her friend. "So we were right? They really did it?"

Lou turned to Easton, who shook his head in disbelief.

But it was Roy who spoke up. "You were right, Lou. Elise was mad about Arthur not stepping down. She swears that she only went to confront him, but he blew her off and made her feel so helpless that when he climbed down from the ladder to grab a tool from his truck, she used the time to climb up and expose the wires in a few places on the section he was working on. When he returned and still wouldn't listen to her, she walked over to the transformer box, unlocked it, and turned it on."

Easton swallowed. "She said she was only trying to give him a shock, to scare him into believing that he shouldn't be running the company any longer. But he fell, got tangled in the lights, and ended up getting continually shocked until his heart stopped."

"She didn't realize Ferris had seen her running from the scene of the crime until he came to her and Chandler that night with her phone she'd dropped as she ran away," Roy said, picking up the story from there. "Apparently, her purse got stuck on the fence and while she was trying to yank it free, her phone flew out. He said he wanted money to stay silent.

"Chandler and Elise said they agreed to the blackmail, but when Chandler went to meet him the following day to drop off the first installment of money, he said he got so angry and ended up attacking Ferris instead."

At that moment, the local aid car pulled up. They moved Olivia from the car into the ambulance, letting Lou ride along with her as they took her to the hospital to make sure she didn't have any lasting effects from sitting in a cold shed for forty-eight hours.

Lou watched her friend with disbelief. She was just about to relax when her phone, and Olivia's phone, started ringing at the same time. Lou jumped, realizing she hadn't filled in Willow or her parents on the developments.

Choosing her phone, Lou answered, blurting out, "I'm okay. Olivia's okay. We found the killers, and I'll explain everything," in one breath before they could ask questions.

CHAPTER 24

CHRISTMAS DAY...

Lou sank into her couch, loving the feel of her soft, new flannel Christmas pajamas. She'd had to get rid of a cute pair, featuring reindeer, in order to buy these this year, but it all seemed worth it.

Everything was perfect. A fire crackled away in the hearth, Lou's parents were seated across from her, wearing matching sets of pajamas, Christmas music played softly in the background, and Willow was on her way. Lou and her parents sipped at coffees while they waited, gifts stacked under the tree. Sapphire was curled up, asleep in Lou's lap. Catnip Everdeen had continued her acceptance of Bruce. Charles Lickens and Anne Mice were fighting for the prime spot on Caroline's lap in the coziest competition Lou had ever witnessed.

"Hello," Willow called as she bustled into the apartment.

"Merry Christmas," the Welsh family called out in greeting.

A few gift bags hung from Willow's right arm, and she had a cardboard box tucked under the other.

"I just got off the phone with my parents," Willow said as she set down the box and brought the gift bags over to the Christmas tree. "They say hello," she relayed as she set down her gifts.

Lou beamed. "So do the Henrys."

They'd chatted with Maddy, Mia, Joey, and Emily earlier via video call. Ben's brother and his family had a foot of new snow and were probably in the middle of a snowball fight now that they were done with the call.

Willow snapped her fingers. "I missed talking to the girls?"

While Willow had met Lou's nieces a handful of times over the course of their lives, she'd really grown close to them during their stay with Lou that summer.

"I think you talk to them more than I do these days," Lou said, knowing Willow had been sending them pictures and videos of the new nursery space. "Okay, are we ready for presents?" Lou clasped her hands together with excitement.

"Beyond ready," Willow said, plopping down in the armchair across from Lou.

"First, how did Easton like your gift?" Lou asked, pulling her elbows tight to her body in anticipation.

Willow's eyes lit up. "He loved it. It was a big hit, and…"

"And…?" Lou leaned closer.

"He gave me the sweetest sign that has Willow's Nursery carved into the wood." She pressed her lips together, holding back her beaming smile as much as she could.

Caroline placed a hand over her heart. "That's so sweet."

"Um." Bruce glanced from Caroline to Lou, then stage-whispered, "He does know that's not going to be the name of her nursery, right?"

Lou couldn't blame her dad for wondering. Willow's business was going to be called Valley Nursery, since she wanted to highlight that the plants were all being sourced from a farm in the Skagit Valley.

"That's the really sweet part," Willow said, swooning. "Apparently, he made it for me years ago. I must've mentioned my dream of owning a nursery to him when we were still just neighbors, and he made it, saying he knew I would make it happen someday."

Caroline let her head fall back into the couch like she was melting from the cuteness of it all.

"Well done, Easton." Lou nodded in appreciation.

"He loved the garden net too. I think he's setting it up right now." Willow smirked. "OC was helping him when I left."

Lou chuckled. As much as Easton and Willow's horse had gotten off on the wrong foot at the beginning of their relationship, they'd grown quite close over the past few months.

"Well, here's your gift, Willow." Lou set a wrapped box in front of her best friend.

Willow pointed since Lou was already standing by the tree, ready to hand out presents. "The green one's for you, Lou. And the red is for Care Bear and Bruce."

Bruce stood so he could hand out their presents. Once all the gifts under the tree were divided up, they opened one at a time.

There were hand-knit socks, hanging plants, books, pottery, and blankets strewn around the room once the presents were opened. Lou felt a warmth radiate from her chest, and she couldn't help but smile as she sat there with the people she loved most in the world.

Her phone buzzed with an incoming call, and she saw it was Olivia. She accepted the call, surprised to see it was a video link. Behind the author, Chuck stood in the kitchen chopping vegetables, no doubt preparing his famous Christmas stew.

"Merry Christmas!" Olivia waved.

Lou scooted around so the camera would catch Willow, Caroline, and Bruce in the background too. "Merry Christmas," they said in response.

Olivia had been home for almost a week. It had taken her a few days to get cleared by the hospital—one of her little toes had been very close to frostbite—and for her to give her statements to the police. Chuck had been more than happy to have her home. He was even more grateful when he learned the truth behind her not making it to her signing in Portland, flying out to meet her in Seattle, so she didn't have to make the trip home alone.

Olivia's gaze moved to the wrapping paper strewn across the living room. "Oh, good. You've opened presents. Bruce and Caroline, what do you think?" Her voice rose in pitch—as much as a serious ex-New York cop's could, anyway.

Bruce held up his socks. "We love the gifts," he said, the words almost sounding more like a question.

Olivia narrowed her eyes. "You haven't done it yet." The video of her cut out while she must've flattened it against her sweater. "I think I just messed up," she whispered to Chuck.

"We can still hear you, even if you can't see us," Lou teased.

Olivia's face reappeared on the video screen. She smiled way too big and let out a strangled laugh.

"It's okay. I was just about to unveil the surprise." Lou stood, handing the phone off to Willow. "Here, you can watch." Lou walked over to the kitchen table, stopping at the cardboard box Willow had brought with her.

What Bruce and Caroline couldn't see from across the room was that the top of the box had sizable holes cut out of it. Inside, a cozy blanket had been folded up, and a small black cat with a white mustache was fast asleep, curled into a little ball.

Lou opened the box, pulling out the familiar kitten.

"Goose?" Bruce jumped to his feet.

Caroline gasped. "Oh, Lou, did the people who adopted him bring him back?"

Lou shook her head, walking over with the purring bundle. "I was the one who adopted him. I just told you it was someone else. Noah brought him to Willow's for me, and she's been keeping him at her house for me for over the past two weeks."

Bruce stopped a few feet away from his daughter, frowning. "Why would you do that?"

"Because," Lou said, "I got him for you."

"Lou, this ... I can't—" It was the second time in so many weeks she'd seen her dad truly speechless.

Caroline got to her feet and rushed over. "Oh, Goose. What do you say? Do you want to be our travel buddy?" She reached forward to take the kitten from Lou.

He blinked open his gorgeous green eyes and rubbed his head on Caroline's chin before cuddling up to her neck, looking like he might fall asleep again.

"That little guy is seriously the sleepiest cat I've ever met. He can sleep through anything, even a goat prancing around and bleating loudly when he thinks his breakfast is late." Willow rolled her eyes.

"He's perfect. Thank you, honey." Caroline pulled Lou in for a side hug, careful not to disturb the sleeping cat.

Bruce swallowed, finally seeming like he was coming to his senses. He pulled Lou in for a side hug as well, staring at the kitten. "Inconceivable," he whispered in awe.

"I do not think that means what you think it means," Olivia supplied the following line from *The Princess Bride* from the phone across the room, reminding them she was still connected.

"Oh, Olivia, sorry, I forgot you." Lou raced over and took the phone from Willow, who'd kept it pointing out, so Olivia had seen all the action.

"Don't worry, sweetie. I'm glad they like the gift, and that I didn't ruin it. I'll talk to you later, okay? Tomorrow I have a new book to start." She gave her a salute.

"Let me guess," Lou said. "It's all about a Scrooge-like character getting murdered by a string of Christmas lights?"

"Bingo." Olivia cackled as she hung up the call.

Once she tucked her phone away, and they'd all returned to their seats in the living room, Bruce drew in a long breath and said, "Well, you all realize what this means, don't you?"

Based on her father's movie quote moments before, Lou guessed, "You want to watch the movie again?"

Bruce scratched underneath the kitten's chin. "With a perfect mustache like this, I think we might have to change his name to Inigo," Bruce said, bringing up Mandy Patinkin's character in *The Princess Bride*. "*And* maybe we should watch the movie just one more time, to be sure."

"Dinner's prepped. We just have to put a few things in the oven. But that can wait." Caroline snuggled closer to Bruce and the kitten on the couch.

"I'm in," Willow said, curling her feet under her and grabbing the cozy blanket Lou had just given her.

"Sure thing, Dad. As you wish." Lou grabbed the remote control, pulled Sapphire into her lap, and settled in for a perfectly cozy Christmas Day.

Finding a body in your nursery is kind of a big dill.

It's grand opening time for Willow's nursery. Louisa's best friend is brimming with nerves. It doesn't help that her beloved pygmy goat, Steve, has recently gone missing. To make matters worse, on the morning of her first day of business, Willow shows up to find her front gate wide open. She should be worried if anything has been stolen, but she's somewhat more concerned with the body lying cold in the middle of the succulents.

When the victim is identified as an auditor for the department of agriculture with documentation showing Willow was in possession of plants prohibited for sale in the state, the local police look at her as their prime suspect even though she swears the plants aren't hers. But Willow wasn't the only one who had reason to want the auditor out of the way, and Lou might have to venture into Brine, the pickle-themed town next door, to find allies and prove her friend's innocence.

Buy it now!

Join Eryn Scott's mailing list to learn about new releases and sales!

About the Author

Eryn Scott lives in the Pacific Northwest with her husband and their quirky animals. She loves classic literature, musicals, knitting, and hiking. She writes cozy mysteries and women's fiction. Join her mailing list to learn about new releases and sales!

www.erynscott.com